Behind the Eyes

Sharon K. Angelici

2025 ©

Write with Light Publications, Colorado, USA
ISBN: 978-1-7378158-8-4
ISBN: 978-1-970289-01-5
ISBN: 979-8-3382822-3-6
Library of Congress Number: 2024946026

If you know me, you'll understand in my heart
Love is the answer.
Always
Love.

In the story of *Behind the Eyes* you will meet this lovely cast of characters and travel to these places. This is how they sound in my head:

Isolde: ĩz-ōld, ĩz
Rasabel: rã-zã-bẽl, rã-zā, bẽl
Bylyn: bī-lĩn
Intan: ĩn-tãn
Fleur: flũr

Mondurey: mãn-dẽr-ā
Acadia: ã-kā-dē-ã

Table of Contents

CHAPTER ONE

The downy pillow beneath Isolde's head was soft against her skin, and the air carried the scent of blooming magnolias. She smiled as she rolled toward the stunning colors of the morning's sunrise. "Twenty-eight has arrived," she squealed with a smile. "I wonder what Uncle Bradford will add to the armory for me?"

She lay for a long moment, thinking about her age. As far back as she could remember, her uncle had given her a weapon of defense to celebrate her birthday. It was predictable, the blossoming tree as she woke and the afternoon spar with an unexcited training partner, but she treasured it all.

The real challenge of her age was the lack of a ring on her marriage finger. She had no desire to be owned by a woman or a man. She also understood that time to make that decision for herself was running out. Commitment or convent would be her choices, but not this morning.

"Today I will enjoy my birthday." She flopped on her back, appreciating the intricate details of her chamber ceiling — the painted hues of a rising sun gobbling up the night sky. She loved the warmth of the sun, especially when it broke through her bed-chamber window.

She kicked herself from the bed and with more enthusiasm than usual she readied herself for a morning of swordplay and perhaps some celebratory fun.

"Where is everyone?" she asked as she strolled through the dining hall. There were no gifts on the table, nor Evangeline to help with breakfast, which was odd and a little upsetting. She wandered beyond the stables to the armory shed.

"Happy birthday to me," Isolde sing-songed as she prepared to pull her gear from the building. The practice dummy was always first. It was the heaviest burden and once it was set in the training circle she could choose her weapon.

"Are you talking to yourself, dear?" Her uncle was inches shorter than her and rounder in the belly than he'd been in years, but he was kind and almost never forgot important things.

Isolde jumped, startled by the break in silence. "You frightened me, Uncle."

"Good morning," he said, pleased that he'd snuck up on his usually aware niece.

"It is a good morning." She noticed his unsteady pace as he leaned against the training room threshold.

"A special day for you." He kissed her as she returned to the shed. "Twenty-eight, today." He coughed, the sound deep and long lasting.

She paused to scrutinize his trembling. "Are you feeling unwell?" she asked.

He waved off her concerns. "I'll be fine. I'm savoring the day with you."

"I enjoy your company," she said, removing her practice sword, "but it is unlike you to miss birthday breakfast."

She tapped her sword against the thatched training dummy. The armored scarecrow meant to represent an enemy held no weapons, so the girl practiced swinging her blade and controlling her body to prevent a single touch to the wicker silhouette.

"Are you worried for me or for your present?" he teased. He'd planned her gift for months, sending secret correspondence and negotiating deals to make this a special experience that would last for a lifetime.

"I'll admit I was excited for a new training weapon, but your wellness worries me."

He watched her exercise with the blade, impressed by her posture, but also noting her limited experience with fighting. "I will be fine."

"If you say so. I guess I have to trust you to tell me the truth." Isolde paused when her uncle sat.

"I have something special for you this year," he explained. "I have sent for someone to train with you."

"Is it another sloppy boy in rusty armor?" Isolde's blade tip sliced the single shaft of straw sticking from her target's jugular area.

Uncle Bradford chuckled, teasing her with the details about his surprise. "It is no boy, dear. It is the bishop's Captain of the Guard."

Isolde's curiosity was piqued.

"I knew you'd approve." He grinned. Pleased with himself, he continued. "Expect the captain's arrival by nightfall in two days and then perhaps you will meet your match."

She settled her gray eyes on him. "I will meet my match only in a different lifetime." She chuckled. "You ask for teachers, Uncle, and they send boys who will not fight me after two days." She continued practicing her sword handling. "But they have no problem suggesting where to put their daggers." She made a thrusting gesture with her hips.

"Don't be crude, Isolde," her uncle scolded.

"It isn't my crudeness that is the problem, Uncle." She rested her sword atop the storage hooks. "They are arrogant." She adjusted her sun-bleached hair, trying to gather the distracting stray strands so they would not break her focus. She picked up a bow.

"Arrogant, really?" he mocked. "You don't say." He knew his niece was talented in a fight—better than every trained person in Mondurey, he was almost certain. She was assertive in her convictions, but she was also fighting against a world that saw her beauty first, and that obstacle was an impossible foe.

She nocked the arrow against the bowstring, locking it into firing position. "Do not confuse my confidence with arrogance, Uncle." She drew the bowstring against her right cheek, taking one deep breath before letting it slip free. The feather fletching cut through the air, hitting the target left of center. "Men don't like strong women. That is why I'll never lower myself to take their hand"—she turned to him with a mischievous grin—"except maybe to pick it up when I sever it from their wrist."

"Isolde!" he scolded. "I am fully aware you'll take no man into your life." He grimaced, feeling a sharp pain in his side but hiding it from his niece.

"Or into my bed." She grinned, switching her handhold and nocking another arrow.

Her uncle covered his ears, afraid to hear what else might come out of her mouth. "Please, child, I am too old to hear your stories and count your conquests."

"If it is possible for you to count my so-called conquests, perhaps you should stop calling me a child." She loosed the second arrow into the center of the target. "I will be the lady of this house, and one day you won't be able to call me child." Satisfied with the new bow string, she returned it to the rack on the wall.

"I'll make the alteration when you stop acting like one."

She ignored his comment as she adjusted the bracer around her forearm. For her next exercise she chose a longer, heavier blade, and tipped it against the heart of her practice dummy. "Two days, you say?" She turned as she asked the question. "For the captain to arrive?"

"Two days." He walked away seconds before she plunged the blade through the heart of her imaginary enemy. "You will finally meet your match, dear girl."

Isolde smiled, excited for the gift but not expecting much of a challenge. "I look forward to sending the captain all the way back to Acadia."

"Ah." He turned around. "Look behind the fletching stand. There's a gift for you there."

She loosened her grip on the sword handle and spun toward the armory door. He wasn't her father by blood but he was in spirit, and if she had to choose she would pick him.

The box of feathers and pitch on the fletching table were off center; she should have noticed. When she pushed them aside, she found six stones resting on a leather bundle. "Rocks?" She studied them for special features, gemstone quality or something to make them stand out as a gift. She lined each on the table, resigned that none were particular treasures. Without the weight of the stones, the bundle unfolded and Isolde smiled. She'd learned the technique of sling hunting from him, kind of. It was a fond birthday memory….

"It's going to clunk your head," he said as she tucked the stone in the pocket.

"You have no faith, Uncle Bradford." She used the energy of her nine-year-old arm to twirl the sling. She felt the weight pull against the finger loop wrapped around her finger. Before she was ready, the hold knot released, launching the stone straight up. Her uncle dove away, predicting almost exactly what would occur.

Isolde did not move, surrendering to her fate as the stone plopped on the ground at her feet. "That was a terrible first try."

"As predicted," her uncle said and chuckled, brushing the dirt from his clothes.

Intent to excel at this new challenge, Isolde tucked another rock into the pocket. "I know what I did wrong." She repeated her previous attempt, adding a flick in her wrist. The stone did not release but instead smacked the back of her shoulder. She looked to her uncle for approval before picking up the rock once more. "There is no victory without defeat."

"Good attitude, my girl."

Feeling encouraged, she balanced the cord ends from the center. She made two more attempts, each with small, but failing, adjustments.

"I think I'm going to leave you to practice," her uncle said, using the drape of his coat sleeve as head cover while he escaped from the practice field.

Now, almost 20 years later, Isolde rubbed the braided cord between her fingers. A gilded thread ran through the twist—surely not gold, but still splendid to hold. The pocket was thick leather, subtle enough to keep the stone in place. It was a thoughtful gift. Something to treasure as she grabbed the rocks and returned to the practice yard.

She kissed the first stone for luck, tucked it in the pocket and twirled the sling. The sound was unmistakable as she circle-stepped to find a target. The Mondurey banner hung on the courtyard wall. It was perfect at more than twenty meters. The knot slipped through her fingers, launching the stone across the courtyard, hitting the banner near the center of her family crest.

"Bravo!"

She spun around to see her uncle standing on the balcony bridge. Her smile was impossible to hide. "I had an excellent teacher."

~~~~~~~~~~

Days later, the courier arrived with another cord-bound parchment bearing the bishop's sacred waxed seal over the folds. "There are still more to come," the courier said as he back-stepped to leave Isolde in the mourning chamber.

Two days had passed since her birthday celebration, but now she was planning a burial. Isolde stared at the body on the bed, her hands as cold as her emotions when she broke the official seal on the letter. She was not a weak woman, but the words in the letter made her head dizzy. Her gaze drifted between her uncle's body and the sentiment of the correspondence. "How?" she cried.

Feeling betrayed, she tucked the message inside her belt. "Uncle, what has happened?" She despised his corpse, thinking she could not mourn a man who sacrificed her future to appease a god she did not abide; a god he no longer knelt before.

"How could you do this to me, Uncle?" His face was painted and he no longer looked like the man who had raised her; like the man who'd treated her as his own, but secretly traded her to save himself after death.
~~~~~~~~~~

"My family name gave you everything, and you do this to me." She read the first sentence of the new letter. "After confirming Bradford of Mondurey's passing, the bishop insists the property of the land transfer to Acadia's holdings, along with the unwed niece as payment for unresolved debts." She tucked the paper into her belt and slapped her heart. "I am not an unresolved debt." She fought back tears. "What have you done?"

In the days to come, she feared the life she knew and the land she called home would transfer from an uncle who made promises on her behalf to the Bishop of Acadia who referenced her in ways no man of god should speak.

The old man's death could have been natural or masterfully-planned foul play. She would never know, but the arrival of such a letter could not have been done in haste. "Did the bishop grow tired of waiting to own me?" she asked his corpse.

Her life was unconventional from the moment she took her first steps. She defied boundaries, breaking from traditional roles for a lady; she hunted, practiced armored riding and trained with a sword. Before this twenty-eighth birthday, she had bested every training partner for miles. Isolde would fight this destiny, too.

"Your gift to me," she cried, "this captain you sent for… he will arrive in time to attend your funeral, Uncle." She expected everything to change. "I fear the captain's motives are beyond training. Now that you're gone, his loyalties will lie with the bishop's desires."

She buttoned the collar of his funeral shirt. He would lay for another day, allowing the people of the land to pay their respects. Isolde wished it could be different. Without the guidance and protections of her uncle, her freedom was lost.

As the day faded to night, Isolde learned of the captain's arrival but did not leave her chamber. Her heart ached for the loss of so much, and she could not bear to spend her evening with another man.

CHAPTER TWO

The afternoon sun was warm as Rasabel adjusted the pauldron on her shoulder. The Acadian insignia stamped in the leather marked her place in the town, but also implied her status in the Bishop's guarding forces. She answered to no one aside from the holy man.

This day was like so many others, as she teased her best friend, Anwar, who aspired to be her second in command. "You must shuffle." She moved her feet through the dirt, sliding with intent to prevent kicking up dust. She wasn't boastful in her technique—she was teaching what she loved and was always interested in making her students better.

"Stop it, Rasa," he argued. "You can't correct me every time." They stood toe to toe. They were similar in height and build but not at all alike as fighters.

"Anwar, my friend"—Rasa added the term of endearment to soften her next words—"your footwork gives me an advantage and is also terribly sloppy."

He frowned, knowing she was right but hating that she was right. "Is it possible for us to spar and only spar?"

"You will fall." She tapped her sword against his to signal readiness. They knew each other well, but she didn't understand why he resisted her techniques. "Be at the ready."

"You are always so sure." He clomped his boot on the ground and she sidestepped easily, spinning to smack his backside with the flat of her blade. "Stop playing, Rasa."

"Start fighting like you want to be my second."

He shrugged her insult away and advanced with the same horrible technique.

She repeated her reaction, this time smacking him twice as hard.

"Rasa," he yelled.

She chuckled. "How will you learn? If you will not listen, I must show you what awaits you if you meet a foe as schooled as I am." She heard footfalls against the stone path. One approached, light on their feet.

"Captain," the courier interrupted and Rasa spun toward his voice. "Important orders from the bishop."

~~~~~~~~~~

Rasa tossed her gloves against the armory wall, the orders from the Bishop leaving her too frustrated to train with Anwar.

"Might I help with your gear?" Anwar asked, ducking quickly to avoid the pair of gloves flying very near his face.
~~~~~~~~~~

"I am not a babysitter," she insisted as she tucked her heel against the "U" of the boot jack, kicking her foot free from her dirty training boots.

"No, Captain." Anwar stood at attention, knowing when it was best not to address her casually. "You are most certainly not a babysitter."

"And what does a highborn woman need with the skills I teach to my best armed fighters?"

"I don't know, Captain."

Rasa looked up, her stare icy and intimidating. "Anwar, I'm going to ask you to return to your barracks."

"Yes, but if I may?" He took a step backward, uncertain if his next question was safe to ask.

"What is it?"

"Don't you think if the bishop wants *you,* there must be a reason?"

She had pondered that same question as she'd ended their training session. "I don't know. All I do know is that I should be here in Acadia and not playing teacher to some woman."

"I'll be happy to step in while you're away," he teased.

Rasabel turned around, pretending to look for a knife in her back. "You wound me, Anwar. Do you think I'm so easily replaced?"

"No, my friend." He patted her shoulder. "You are irreplaceable to the city and to the rest of the soldiers at your command."

"Thank you," she said.

"You're welcome. I will ensure the rest of the guards understand your assignment."

"I appreciate your support." Rasa unfastened the button on her trousers. "Close the door as you leave."

He knew when he was being dismissed and didn't say another word as he secured the armory.

Rasa unfastened the buckle on her pauldron and draped her clothing over the hooks on the wall. She didn't often study her body unclothed, but at her age, and after so many battles to protect Acadia, she knew the scars were almost too many to count.

"You'll take no wounds caring for a highborn in her tower." She rubbed the rippled skin on her hip. "Babysitter indeed."

~~~~~~~~~~

Rasabel kicked her boot against the rail outside the cathedral, using a bit of spit to shine the scuff on the toe away. It wasn't Sunday, but it was time for obligatory confessions before setting out on an assignment. This holy place did not speak to her and she lingered too long outside trying to put off the inevitable. Her beliefs in the old goddesses prevented communion, and doubled the wrath expected if the bishop's god had his way with her, so she kept her devotions a secret between herself and the confessor waiting inside.

She swept away the hood covering her face and tossed the long braid of dark hair over her shoulder. She stood before the confessional booth, anticipating the struggle it would be to contort her body inside. The confines of the space were a fitting torture for one who showed up to appease a religion she followed out of obligation. She drew the curtain away to thread herself into the booth.
~~~~~~~~~~

The privacy door slid open. "I am here for your confession," the voice said.

"I am a sinner, Father, forgive me," Rasa said, without feeling the truth in a single word. "It has been too many days since my last confession." She was honorable by choice, committed to her leadership duties, and also on occasion lusted after women. Her goddess blessed such pairings so she too felt it as divine—a woman who loved bodies like her own, soft where necessary and warm on cold nights. How she cherished all of her nights.

"What is your sin, child?" the voice behind the dividing wall asked.

"I've been ordered to the house of Mondurey to train the bishop's next conquest," Rasabel grumbled as she worked her thick muscled legs into a position as close to kneeling as she could get.

"This is not your sin, child," he said, knowing Rasa had more than an assignment to confess.

"It's beneath me." The leather of her gloves squeaked as she gripped the kneeler handle, her broad shoulders hunching to fit inside the cramped space. She twisted her hair in a knot, wishing more than anything for the freedom to flee this obligatory torture.

Father Intan knelt behind the confessional wall. He was an unkempt man with mostly good intentions, but impatience with the monotony of his commitment wore on his soul. He longed for a life outside the confines of these pastoral duties. "I understand the transfer is temporary," he said.

"Most things in life are temporary, aren't they, Father?" she joked.

He chuckled, knowing she would respond this way. "I suppose they are."

"I haven't spent these ten years training my people for combat to become a teacher to a spoiled highborn girl. It's a waste of my time and my training." Rasa's confidence at thirty-eight shone through as she complained about her assignment. "I do not want to be a teacher to spoiled highborns, Father Intan. I'm the Captain of the Guard."

"Rasa, you *are* Captain of the Guard, which means you will always be a teacher."

She leaned out the open wall confessional, drawing the curtain away to look at the man. "You're supposed to keep my name out of things when I confess to you."

He tugged the curtain from her hand. "And you are supposed to follow orders and fight the urge to blaspheme." He waved a blessing hand in front of the dividing screen. "Give me strength," he whispered before saying, "Go pray for patience, Rasa, and follow the bishop's orders. There's a new path ahead and if you give it a chance, perhaps it will serve you and you'll enjoy it."

Rasabel exited the confessional. "Enjoy it," she said as she knelt. For the next few minutes she prayed to her war goddess, an action that would be blasphemous to the citizens kneeling beside her. She believed in many deities, but not in the one the Bishop of Acadia followed.

As always, she found comfort in her meditations. She left the church confident she could mind the rules of her confessor, and honor her vow to serve the bishop. Perhaps she could speak prayerfully to her goddess as she rode through the countryside and ask for patience as she arrived at her new assignment.

CHAPTER THREE

Isolde was awake with the rooster's crow, daylight barely breaking across her chamber ceiling. She thought of her uncle, his passing and the requirement for her relocation to Acadia that would arrive with the Captain of the Guard. The frustrating truth was that she could not use a sword or bow to escape her fate, and she dreaded leaving the life she knew in Mondurey. If not for the absence of a ring on her finger, the property and all its memories would have been hers.

She was informed of the captain's arrival late the night before and this morning she was preparing to fight, ready to take her frustrations out on a person who might be a challenge. Isolde dressed in her favorite fighting gear; leather worn to perfect softness, like a second skin, for agility, but thick enough to protect from an aggressor. "Perhaps I will teach this Captain of the Guard a few things." She chuckled as she made a stabbing motion at her reflection in the tall mirror.

She laced her calf-high boots, knowing how much it bothered some that she preferred the freedom of trousers over the confines of skirts.

Her uncle's chair sat empty in the dining hall, and she hurried to eat her porridge. *Why did his gift have to be in the shadow of death?* she thought. *And where is this captain?* It was another level of heartache to dine alone, and she decided she would eat her breakfast in the courtyard as long as she stayed in Mondurey.

She wandered to the practice arena but the captain was not there. Surely he'd received her request to begin this morning. Disappointed in his tardiness, she opened the armory shed door to drag the dummy out into the yard, but the dummy was gone.

"Are you looking for this?" a voice asked.

Isolde leaned through the archway, confused by the location of her overstuffed practice target, and angered by the sword blade buried to the cross-guard where a human's heart would be.

"Is that my sword?" She checked the wall of her armory shed. "That's my sword. Who are you to touch my sword?"

"Apparently I am to be your keeper."

"Apparently?" Isolde repeated, curious to see the face of the voice that sounded less like a soldier and more like a bar wench. "Show yourself," she demanded.

"You're *my* commander, now?" Rasabel teased as she stepped from behind the dummy, drawing the sword from its imaginary heart with celerity Isolde could not help but admire.

Isolde circled the stranger, assessing the guard from head to toe. Broad shoulders were trapped beneath the drape of a warrior's cloak. The woman was sturdy, covered in snug-fitting fighting pants and thick leather chest armor. This woman was not the captain she expected, and she liked what she saw.

The captain flexed her sword arm, making it clear she could hold the position and never tire.

This one would be fun to best in a fight and doubly exciting to take to my bed, Isolde thought, but dared not show her interest. "You are the captain of the bishop's guard?" she asked.

"I am. Captain Rasabel of Gladeview, and as of today I am also your teacher." The captain did not bow or submit. She twirled the sword, rotating a large circle before flipping to reverse the blade so the smaller woman could take it from her.

There was nothing special about the practice weapon, but it belonged to Isolde. "And how will you educate me, teacher?" Perhaps it was her melancholy, or the woman's brazen pauses, but Isolde didn't appreciate the surveying glances the captain returned.

"I will teach, as per your uncle's request," the captain said.

"So you are here to show me how to defeat you?" Isolde felt the weight of her weapon as the captain released it. "As per my uncle's deal," she corrected.

The captain stepped back, instantly aware of the anger in Isolde's tone and expecting aggression. "I understand there are changes to my original contract. This arrangement is only different as I must follow the bishop's orders before your uncle's request."

It was not the plan gifted to her two days ago. The captain was more than a teacher now; she was also her keeper. "My life is about to become more complicated," Isolde admitted.

"I'm at your service." Rasa dipped her head.

Isolde studied their closeness separated by the blade in her hand. "For how long?"

Rasa felt the energy change. Whatever this woman was thinking, it brought a wicked grin to her face. "I'll train you to fight until you best me with your sword."

"And after that?" Isolde chuckled. "Did my uncle tell you to best me in the bedroom, too?"

Rasabel took a step backward. "He did no such thing, and—"

"And?" Isolde interrupted.

"I'm here to train you, and there will be nothing more."

Isolde ran her fingertip across the woman's leather-armored chest. "That's terribly unfortunate, Captain."

Rasa grabbed Isolde's hand. "Then the rumors are true?"

Isolde tugged her hand free, confusion rising inside her. "Rumors?"

"Not rumors so much as observations that you have now confirmed."

Isolde raised her sword; she was tired of the verbal sparring and needed to expend some of her confusing emotions. "And what would these rumors and observations be?"

Rasa smiled and the tiny scar beneath her eye creased into a misshapen dimple. "It is said you tangle with women of the old ways and that you prefer their comfort at night."

Isolde tipped her chin, and she held her head proudly. They stood face to face, Isolde a few inches shorter but equal in confidence, her blade tip circling in the space between them. "I find what I need when I need it, and I never need the comfort of men. I make no apologies for who I am because they are not choices—they are only me."

The captain's smile was brief. "Then you will find we have more in common than swords and arrows." Her response was fluid and in a blink she drew a sword from her back, ready to defend.

"Do we?" Isolde's feet moved through the dry surface of the sparring ring with such smooth motion, that barely any dust rose at her feet.

Rasa was patient, feeling matched for the first time as she waited for the woman to advance.

~~~~~~~~~~

"I grow tired of the monotony," Isolde said as she finished the porridge. It had been weeks of talking about tactics and techniques, and less of the action of it. She wanted more than words as they trained.

Rasabel chuckled. "You have excellent skills with a sword, and your accuracy with a bow is impressive." She took the empty bowl from Isolde and set it on the courtyard
~~~~~~~~~~

serving table. "If you shoot a bow, you must know how to string it, and if you hit a target, you must learn to fletch an arrow if it is lost or damaged. These are also skills that matter."

"Why would they matter?" Isolde followed Rasabel to the armory shed. "I will have people to help me if those skills are weak."

"And if you do not?" Rasa asked.

"I'll use my sword."

Rasa pushed the armory door closed, locking Isolde on the opposite side. "You have no weapon, Isolde. What will you do now?" She climbed through the open shutters, landing a few feet from the other woman.

Isolde balled her hand in a fist and threw a powerful, frustrated punch at her teacher.

Rasa anticipated the move, dodging the blow. "Very good."

Isolde smiled. "I missed your face."

Rasa turned her cheek, grinning. "But I felt the breeze and it cooled me down."

"You're mocking me." Isolde stood her ground.

Rasa apologized. "I am merely pointing out that one day you may only have your hands and feet. They will become weapons too."

"I know this," Isolde said.

"Yes, but I want your body to know it without stopping to think."

Isolde scowled. "Was it part of your lesson to make me want to punch your face?"

"Maybe not my face, but in a fight there is no fair and unfair. There is only a winner and a loser, and where I come from, the loser ends up in the ground."

"Where you come from—" Isolde repeated, missing the second part of the sentence as thoughts of her future move crowded her mind. "Acadia?" she asked, sobering at the idea that the town where the bishop lived would become her new home.

Rasabel nodded.

"We are going?"

Rasa nodded again.

"Is there any way to fight it?"

Rasa opened the armory door and Isolde followed. "I promise you will know everything I know. You will have knowledge I do not share with even the best of the guards. This is the only way I can help you fight what is to come."

"Thank you," Isolde said.

"I will try to prepare you for whatever that is." Rasa opened the cabinet. "But you have to trust the way I do it."

"Trust," Isolde whispered. "It does not come easy."

"But it will come." Rasa took the sling from the shelf. "Now we fight with the easiest weapon to find."

"Uncle Bradford," Isolde whispered.

Rasa's brow furrowed. "What did you say?"

Their hands touched as Isolde took the sling. She felt her heart strings pull toward the captain, trying to fight the attraction. This captain could be nothing more, as her true task was to take Isolde to her terrible future. Focusing on the leather and twine in her hands, she explained, "This was a gift from my uncle."

"He gave you a sling?" Rasa was immediately curious about such a present.

"Not only a sling, but the techniques to use it." The leather was supple in her hand. Tears formed as Isolde realized it was the last thing she'd received from him before his betrayal.

"A very wise man," Rasa said. "This is the easiest weapon to make when you have nothing else." She opened the pouch on her hip, removing her own sling. "Are you up for a challenge?"

Isolde smirked. "You should know I am very good."

"I would not expect anything else."

~~~~~~~~~~

"I do not wish to leave here." Isolde said as she mounted her horse. The weeks of uninterrupted training had turned to months, until the bishop grew tired of his new ward's independence. The power struggle would tip in his favor now as they mounted for the two-day ride.

Rasa looked ready for battle in her full captain's uniform. "I have advised the bishop that you wish to remain in Mondurey, but—"

"But I belong to Acadia now." Isolde tapped her heels against the horse and the animal began a slow trot through the gate. She resented being treated like a thing.

"I am sorry, Isolde," Rasa said, riding by her side.

"It's not your doing." They approached the cemetery. "I would like to say goodbye."

"Of course. We have plenty of daylight." Rasa waved the wagon driver ahead.

Isolde dismounted to walk between the headstones. Her ancestors lay among statues erected to the old gods and goddesses. She set a copper coin atop the marker for the father she'd never known. "I'm told he was a good man."
~~~~~~~~~~

"People don't waste time making up stories of goodness." Rasa stood beside her. "So if he was known that way, it was probably so."

Isolde tucked her hand in the crook of Rasa's arm and the captain wrapped her fingers atop. It was meant to console but the women felt more than consolation in the touch.

"You are surprisingly good, Captain."

"Is that so?" Rasa teased.

"I wouldn't dare tell a falsehood about you." Isolde released their hold, wandering behind the headstone to where her mother lay.

Rasa approached moments later, a flower in hand. "For her," she offered.

Isolde laid it across her mother's name. "I never knew either of them. I have no face to put with their titles, yet I miss them the most."

"It is an unbearable sorrow with or without a face to remember."

"You have lost your own?"

Rasabel nodded.

"You don't speak of yourself very much, Captain." Isolde emphasized the formal title. "Do you fear that I will know you too well?"

"I fear few things, Isolde of Mondurey." Rasa grinned, throwing her official title back at the woman. "You knowing me too well will never be one of them."

Isolde turned to look at her. "Very bold, Captain."

"Yes, I believe we are."

Isolde leaned closer to the armored woman and they stood for a long time, thoughts about the future and the past swirling together to make a present neither quite understood.

Their final stop was the freshly-set dirt-covered gravestone of Isolde's uncle. "His death was too soon." She did not fight the tears. "My feelings about him are conflicted," she confessed. "He sold me to the highest bidder, but he also brought you to me."

"I am grateful for that second arrangement." Rasa held her hand to Isolde. "And we will combat the bishop's pressures."

"My heart will never belong to that man." Isolde did not dare to look at Rasabel as she placed a copper coin beside her uncle's name. She was attracted to this warrior, to her heart and to the passion she lived every moment of every day. She did not want to imagine their impending separation. Her turn away was abrupt as she left Rasa standing amongst the strangers' headstones.

Grief lingered as Isolde mounted her horse. She could not foresee the direction ahead as she feared the worst at the hands of the holy leader. "Will we train in Acadia?" she asked, adjusting in her saddle.

"Nothing between us will change," Rasa affirmed. "I will make sure of it. I swear."

"Can you make that promise, Captain?" She slipped to the formal use of Rasa's name, trying to put space between her attraction and the truth.

"Isolde." Rasa hurried the horse beside her.

"You must not say my name with such affection," Isolde whispered. "It is like a dagger to my heart."

Rasa held the reins of Isolde's horse. "Do you think I hurt any less?" She touched the woman's chin. "Isolde?"

"I fear I see what I want."

"Which is?" Rasa asked.

"A reflection of what is behind the eyes. The wishes I make in the dark when I want to be with you."

"In the dark." Rasa smiled. "We will find a way."

CHAPTER FOUR

The dust settled around them as Rasa gave her student space to reclaim her weapon. Isolde scoffed as she picked up her sword. "You frustrating woman."

"It only took you five months to figure that out?" Rasa teased, her teeth shining through her shameless smile.

"Ugh," Isolde squawked. "You're impossible." She raised her blade to ready position.

Rasabel tapped the tip of her blade against her opponent's. "You're impatient."

Isolde tapped back a little harder. "Why do you wait so long to advance?"

Rasabel didn't move, her blade steady as she held position. "You attack, I defend. That is how it is done in a fight."

"And if I don't attack?" Isolde puffed a breath at the loose strand of hair covering her eye.

"Then"—Rasa stepped forward, trapping the tip of Isolde's blade beneath her arm—"there is no need for me to defend." The blade fell away as she tucked the hair behind Isolde's ear with a contradictory tender touch.

Isolde felt a surge of excitement in her racing heart. "And if I decide to move when your defenses are down?" She grasped her teacher's throat, their lips a breath apart.

Rasabel rasped. "I might have to rethink my strategy." She chuckled before twisting out of Isolde's grasp.

"You have pleasing strategies." Isolde winked.

Rasa blushed as she waved her blade tip to point. "As do you and your eyes."

Isolde smiled.

"They are like two shining moons, drawing me under a spell."

"The goddess has given me a secret weapon for night and day." Isolde winked again.

"See what you do. You bring a warrior to her knees with a wink and a smile." Rasa touched the flat of her blade to her forehead, as if trying to clear the lustful thoughts from her mind.

"You are falling into my trap, Ras-a-bel," Isolde teased. "What will your strategy be when it is you and me, with all these defenses and strategies gone to the side?"

Rasabel raised her sword to ready position. "When the sun sets, and you close your chamber door, I'll drop all my defenses and find some rest." Her grin was flirtatious.

"Is that a tease for me to visit your bedchamber, Captain Rasabel?" Isolde raised her sword, shuffle-stepping before swinging at her teacher. Gone were the predictable unconscious actions: the shifts in her steps or twitching in her hand-hold.

Rasa defended, feeling the power Isolde had gained in their training together. She was a better fighter now, stronger in every way, but standing toe-to-toe, she still could not best the captain.

"You did not answer." Isolde spun, her blade striking once and again.

Rasa reacted, holding nothing back, the equal exchange fueling her desire. "It is a solemn vow I make, Isolde of Mondurey, that I will be yours until I am no longer able." Her right hand joined her left, preparing to drop a full-force blow.

Distracted by Rasabel's candor, Isolde did not deflect, and the strike knocked her to the ground. They had fought with this intensity since that very first day and never once was the smaller woman so slow to react.

"Isolde," Rasabel called as the sword fell away. She was terrified she had injured her. "Is," she called again, kneeling at Isolde's waist while her trembling hands roamed her body in search of a wound.

Isolde touched Rasa's chin. "What did you say?"

"Is." Rasa's breath hitched.

"Did you make a solemn vow?"

Isolde's voice melted the warrior's soul. As their eyes met, locked on the other, Rasa answered, "Til I am ordered away, or til my death, I will be here for you." She patted her chest, leaving no doubt she meant every word in her heart.

"Get up, you foolish woman." Isolde shoved her playfully, and rested her hand on her muscled shoulder. "You kneel to no one."

"I kneel to the lord bishop," Rasa said as she raised Isolde to her feet. "And I will forever kneel to you."

"Bel," Isolde whispered, her breath heaving, more than any fight could bring about. She tugged at the vibrant silk scarf she'd gifted the captain, pulling them closer to kiss.

"Isolde," Rasa shook her head. "I know my position in the world."

Isolde's fair skin was in sharp contrast beside Rasa's sun-kissed complexion as their fingers tangled together. "Your place is with me."

"And your keeper?" Rasa asked. "The bishop will make demands of you now that we are here in Acadia. Your uncle's debt must be repaid."

"I am no part of his debt," Isolde argued. "The bishop might believe he is the keeper over my eternal soul, but he has no rights to my body."

Rasa laughed. "He is lord of the mighty above. When he learns of our relationship there will be hell to pay."

"I have seen a brief vision of hell living in Acadia," Isolde said.

"Have you?" Rasa raised her eyebrow, her curiosity peaked.

Isolde stepped away from the fighting circle, dragging the warrior into the armory shed with her. What she wanted to share was a secret no one should overhear. "The bishop makes pacts with the devil, while wearing long white robes. His powers confuse most of the people in Acadia."

"I know this, and it is even more reason to use caution," Rasa whispered. She spun them around, lifting Isolde to sit on the table. "We must be careful to guard our affections until I am released of my duty." She held Isolde's hand to her heart. "I love you, Isolde of Mondurey, even if your lands exist no more."

"Love. It is funny to feel love and have it returned," Isolde whispered. "I want more than professions of adoration."

"Is." Rasa kissed Isolde. "We aren't safe to return to Mondurey unless we are wed."

"You know that foul man will never marry us." Isolde held Rasa's hands, needing to touch her. "His plan is to take every bit of what my uncle left behind."

Rasabel hated to acknowledge the truth—she was afraid to give it power, knowing exactly what the outcome would be if Isolde were unprotected. The bishop was a lust-filled monster. "This plan includes you."

Isolde nodded. Since her arrival in Acadia, the bishop insisted on meeting with her one-on-one. It was never in the open, and after every meeting she felt his obsession grow. He was like every other man, wanting to own what was not for sale. "He has said as much during our council sessions. I will be his or I will be—"

Rasa gasped. "That's blasphemy."

"According to his scripture, it's a purification of bloodlines." Isolde scowled.

Rasa was at a loss. Duty demanded she follow the bishop's law, but she could not abide by his violation of Isolde's body. "But he is a holy man."

Isolde shook her head. "He is no such thing."

Rasa tried to pull away, needing to think and pace for focus but Isolde held tight. "You must know someone who would bind our vow? Someone who might help us flee the territory, and live however we dream."

"What freedom is that?" Rasa spat. "Free to sneak and slither about in the dark. How will you survive outside these walls? You've never foraged for a berry in your life."

"I will adapt." Isolde crossed her arms. "I'm not as highborn as you think I am"—she adjusted her posture—"and as promised, you've taught me everything you know."

Rasa's hands trailed up Isolde's body, her gloved hand touching the frown lines beside Isolde's eyes. "You are the highest of those born and I love you, but out there it is not easy."

"In a few weeks, your words of love won't be enough, Bel. Our lives must be bound and until that day we won't truly be safe."

"Calling me Bel does not mean you will get your way." This was not true, Rasa knew. Isolde, in all her ways, possessed Rasa from top to bottom, inside and out, and she was not an unwilling participant. The short version of her name from this woman dissolved the hard facade she maintained. She knew she was losing this fight. "We will be joined in marriage. I swear it." Rasa's kiss was bruising as she released the buckle around her waist, dropping her weapons to the floor.

"How can you be sure?" Isolde fumbled with the buttons at her throat, baring her chest.

"I know someone we can trust." Rasa pulled the shirt over her head, tugging at the ties around Isolde's waist. "He will unite us in marriage and then we will belong only to the other."

Isolde nodded, breathless as Rasa's hand moved beneath the fabric, finding her ready to be taken. Isolde gasped, her legs spreading, welcoming Rasa's touch. "I will be your wife."

Rasabel pulled their bodies together, giving herself to her betrothed. "And I will be yours," she whispered against her breast. "Til death."

Isolde arched against Rasa's lips. "For the rest of my days."

CHAPTER FIVE

"In ya go, little thief." The guard tossed her like a ragdoll, propelling her onto the sludge-covered prison floor.

"It's Bylyn," she yelled toward his retreating backside. "My name is Bylyn and I'm more than a thief." She slapped at the cold metal as she spun against the bars. The guard never divulged why she'd been moved, but she was certain this was the last cage she'd ever occupy. She was one of three women inside, stripped of their clothes and their humanity.

Before Bylyn could say a word, the eldest woman, in the corner, asked, "What'd ya do, little thief?"

Bylyn didn't answer as she studied the corridor along her new prison cage. She'd spent days in the dungeon cellar until they'd brought her up to meet her sentencing official. Death was the order, and Bylyn could not believe it was the price to pay for hunger.

Her long curly locks were cut away, leaving her to look more like a young lad, but without clothes it was clear she lacked the equipment. In a few hours it would not matter what she was. The axe didn't care.

"I asked what ya did," the woman repeated.

"I got caught being hungry," Bylyn said as she stretched through the bars to reach the tattered rag bundled around the piss pot.

"I got caught being hungry too," the third woman said. "Hungry to not have another guard stiff me for my services." She drew her finger beneath her chin, imitating a knife slitting a throat.

Bylyn shuddered. She was in the dungeon of Acadia, the last place she expected to be, for stealing a loaf of bread and picking the pocket of a tunic-free guard.

"I've got to get out of here," Bylyn said as she wrapped the urine-stained cloth around her. The braided cord of the piss pot was in reach as she stretched her thin frame between the bars again. If it wasn't for her head, she might fit through to escape. According to the execution orders, she'd be relieved of it in less than an hour.

"There's only one way out of here, girl." The woman chuckled, mad from obvious starvation and abuse.

Bylyn leaned closer to ask, "How's that?"

"In a bucket of your own blood." Her laugh irritated Bylyn.

"You crone. You might be happy to die in here, but I'm not." The grit on the bar dug into Bylyn's shoulder as she reached the cord. To her surprise, there was a rusted dung knife on the end. She knew what to do with such a thing as she set to work on the cell door lock.

"You're mad, girl, you can't open that with a du—" the woman stopped when the mechanism clicked and Bylyn pushed the cell door open.

"I am mad. Mad as a thief on the run." Bylyn ducked through and pushed the cell door, leaving it cracked enough for her cellmates to use.

She lifted the grate that rested beneath the piss pot's previous location. She knew what the trap door was for and where it led, but it was the only way out.

"Think small," she whispered as she lowered herself through. She crawled away from the danger of the dungeon, covered in the soil of the slum. She'd escape the executioner's wrath carrying little more than stolen rags to cover her body, a rusty dull dagger and a loop of cord tying all of it around her waist.

Bylyn's hands were cold as she snaked herself through the drainage tunnels, a prison cell behind her and the hope for freedom ahead.

Today she was meant to die by the executioner's hand. "No." She covered her ears as the ringing bells from the great hall warned the countryside of a prisoner's escape. "I should have expected that." The noise was loud as it echoed through the tunnels.

The guards had come for her head, but her head was now covered in sludge as she escaped through the sewer. She was gone but not yet free, and now was not the time to stop and think what would happen if they found her. "It brings comfort to know that I can die only once." She felt the thick sludge between her toes.

"Keep going, dunce," she whispered as she squeezed between the gap in the wall. It was the second time in the hour her compact stature was a blessing. She gouged her fingers against the soft earth, carving a way forward but not necessarily out. She could use these marks to backtrack if she needed to. The sludge broke around her body as she slipped through the open space. She clutched the outcropping of stone, desperate to stay above the abyss below.

"Give me a sign, spirits. I'll take any message from any one of you; Goddess of escape, God of rescue, fairies of light and hope—I'm not particular right now." Bylyn's grip gave way and she plummeted ten feet below. She braced to meet solid ground, but instead met the stench-filled pond of septic water. Taking in the gulp of sludge, she fought for a breath of air.

"Ugh." She spat, flailing to rise above the surface. She didn't know how to swim but she also didn't want to die covered in the excrement of strangers. A mass of twigs drifted beside her and she clung to them, letting the flow drag her wherever it might go. Out, she hoped; far from the chase caused by the ringing bells.

"By the goddess and fairies," she said. "Daylight." The tunnel ahead was growing narrow, and she thought it might be her salvation. "Is this the way?" she asked and the angels sang, or perhaps it was the choir—either way, the songs continued until she realized it was the bells vibrating in her ears.

Bylyn kicked her feet as she floundered toward the light, finding a metal gate as her next obstacle. It was large enough for anything but a human to pass through, even one as small as her. The metal was solid, impossible to break with her bare hands, but the lock was like the one in her prison cell. "Thank you, Goddess." She freed the rusted blade from the cord around her waist. "Little thief," she whispered. "This is what you do best."

She threaded her hands between the bars, feeling her way into the keyhole. It was a full circle moment, and the irony was not missed that this was how she found herself in the executioner's path. Picking locks, thievery and resourcefulness got her into and out of the dungeons of Acadia.

Stealing from the lord's guards was the other reason for her imprisonment, but in the end her grumbling stomach was her downfall. The hitch of the pin clicked once and again, springing the mechanism to disengage the lock.

"So easy," she said as the gate swung open, releasing Bylyn and all the trapped debris loose into the river ahead. Her splash was loud, but perfectly timed with the alarm bells summoning the guards searching for her.

She clung beneath the bundle of floating debris, fearful to rise above the surface. Her arm lagged, clutching the dagger and untied rope. She could not see what was around her. Desperate to check her safety, she attempted a peek above the surface. With as much control as she could muster, Bylyn's face breached the water. She was near the bridge leading to the portcullis, and if she stayed calm a little longer she would be free.

"Search for her everywhere," the guard yelled. "She can't get far looking and smelling like the thief that she is."

"Yes, Captain. We won't stop until she's found."

It was almost flattering that the one and only Captain of the Guard was looking for her. Bylyn ducked beneath the bundle again, one hand skimming the bridge wall to guide her away from their search.

Progress was slow as she drifted, afraid to disturb the surface and make herself known. Minutes seemed like hours, but when an opportunity arose she pulled herself from the water, rolled beneath a cart filled with horse dung and hung on with all her strength. The wagon was heading out of the town and that was all she needed to know.

"Stop there," the guard yelled. "What are you carrying?"

"Cleaning the stables, m'lord." The cart driver pulled back the dense fabric covering. "Heaps of dung for the fields."

The guard stepped back, shielding his nose from the odor of the waste pile. "Off with you; make it gone before my captain smells this wretched stench."

"Yes, terribly sorry." The cart driver clicked his tongue and the tired horse continued through the archway and out the palace yard.

Bylyn hooked herself by the crook of her arm, holding tightly as she felt the fear of capture along with the taste of freedom. The axle's steady rotation burned the bare skin of her feet but she did not let go. She was very good at survival.

When she thought she could not hold on any longer, the cart stopped and she dropped to the ground. Wet with river water, she crawled through the straw-covered dirt. Her skin itched from the debris but she continued on her belly.

She found safety in the corner of a pig's sty, finding it ironic that her escape continued to involve a covering of excrement. "You made it, little thief," she whispered, celebrating with herself as she wiped the filth from her body with a fistful of straw.

For the first time in hours she could hear more than the pace of her heart and the blood rushing through her. She could hear the river water pouring over the paddles of the cutter mill's wheel. As much as she hated the idea of getting back into the water, she knew it was a faster way to put distance between herself and the alarm bells ringing through the countryside of Acadia.

She crawled through the stable on her belly, making her way back into the river. *If I'm going to live the life of a thief,* she thought, *I need to learn how to swim.*

The warning bells continued ringing, and Bylyn knew the guards of Acadia wouldn't stop searching until she was found. She passed a cottage as she drifted, and a few moments later there was another. She took it as a sign and crawled from the water, making her way through the brush toward the scent of an outdoor fire; there had to be people, a village or something like it, and perhaps a tiny crumb of food.

A line of clothes hung between tall trees and she snuck close to pull off thread-bare trousers and a well-worn shirt. "The work clothes of a farmer," she whispered. "I've pretended to be a boy before. They'll have to do."

She crept around the building. Manure-covered boots lay outside the door and she snatched the pair. She escaped into the thick of trees as fast as her bare feet could move.

Bylyn stripped away the wet rags she wore and buried them, taking time to smear scent from the dung-coated boots to cover her tracks. Her dungeon stench replaced with that of a farmer would be a perfect change.

The pants were three sizes too wide to go around her and six inches too long at her ankles. At just above five feet tall, it was nearly impossible to find anything to fit her size. She cinched the waist with her cord and stuffed the length of her pants inside the boots. She'd stumble over herself, but at least she would be clothed.

She ran her fingers over her cropped black hair, missing the length. The guards had not shaved it to the skin, like they did most prisoners, but she felt the absence and wanted it covered; a cloak, a scarf—anything to hide her identity.

Bylyn stuck to the forest, using the thicket and weeds to camouflage her path. The further she moved from the prison walls, the quieter the warning bells became.

She could do this. She could find her way to freedom if she stuck to the trees.

CHAPTER SIX

The chill of the night air made Bylyn shiver. "You should have stolen a blanket or a cloak, you idiot," she whispered as she broke through the forest. The inn was closed, but she knew somewhere in this tiny village there would be a place to lay her head.

The wagon-worn path led to a sleepy trading stand. She hoped for a scrap of food, a rotten apple or a piece of bread. There was nothing, not even a rat to catch. The shutters were drawn tight and she wondered if the warning bells of Acadia frightened the residents inside.

Entering homes in the dark wouldn't end well so she didn't dare, but barns and stables were a different story. She'd never been poked by a horse, at least not with a dagger.

She crept among the cows in the barn, snuggling close to a calf for warmth. If only she could share its mother's milk, something to take her belly ache away. She'd close her eyes for a few minutes and move on. She was so tired, but she needed to move on.

~~~~~~~~~~

Bylyn woke to the sounds of barn life, but mostly it was the unending noise of the rooster's crow. Daylight seeped through the cracks of the building walls and she panicked. *I've slept too long,* she thought as she inched to peek through the gap between the sticks of the wall. The yard was quiet, as she crept from the barn, making her way to the canopy-covered dining tables in the courtyard of the inn. She had no coins to pay and no wares to trade, but she had a talented liar's tongue to manipulate a free meal.

The scent of cooking meat was the lure and she hoped somewhere inside she'd find a person willing to give her any portion to satisfy her hunger pains.

"What are you doing there?" the stranger asked.

She jumped, and turned in the direction of his voice. "Looking for a bit to eat. Maybe offer to help clean the barn in exchange for some food."

The man's brow furrowed, confused by the feminine voice coming from the person in men's trousers, and his tone sweetened. He looked more disheveled than Bylyn and his glare was lecherous. "We could take something out in trade."

Bylyn took a large step back, bumping into something or someone.
~~~~~~~~~~

"You'll do no such thing, you old bastard." The innkeeper's voice was gruff, matching her thick, solid, no-nonsense frame. "Come here, child. I'll feed ya, and when you're done eating you can tell me how you ended up here, in the clothing of a farm hand."

Yes, how did I end up here? Bylyn thought. It went farther back than stealing from a guard. It went back to the father who taught her to beg while he sipped at his ale, and the mother who died trying to stop him. She had no place to call home, and no one to guide her to anything but lying, begging and theft.

Bylyn passed a small group of patrons seated for the morning breakfast hour. If she was quick to eat she might find a few treasures in the saddle bags of the horses tied out front. She counted seven and was convinced her pickpocketing prospects had promise.

She could hear the grumble of her empty stomach as the plate was set in front of her. Before she could dip her fingers in for a crisp slice of meat, she heard a voice asking her a question.

"Yes, child. My friends and I are very curious. Tell us how you've come to sit here in the clothes of the hard working?"

She turned, but the glare of daylight obstructed her view of the man and his companions. She saw cloaks that matched the horses' colors, and knew these patrons and the animals belonged together. Her assessment was right; she'd have a pouch of copper before day's end.

"I fell in the river," Bylyn explained. "I thought I would drown with the weight of my dress and shoes, so I kicked them off. I couldn't walk through the village unclothed." She returned to her plate of food.

"Perhaps you shouldn't have fallen in the water," a second voice suggested.

"It was not by choice, I promise you," Bylyn said.

"But you had a choice, didn't you, lit-tle thief?" He drew out the name, as if he knew who she was.

Bylyn heard the rattle of chainmail against the steel of a blade, but she didn't dare turn around. She wouldn't give them the satisfaction. She eyed the piece of salted meat with fondness as she tossed the table over and leaped to safety behind it.

The guard's blade crashed down, inches from her hand, and the only chance at food in days lay in the dirt beside her. She scurried beneath each of the four remaining tables, able to escape one guard after the other. As their cloaks came off, she recognized the uniform symbol from the banner on the wall of the dungeon. With nowhere to run, Bylyn scurried under the platform beneath the woman's workspace. Her oversized boots slipped in the muck as she squirmed and wriggled through the tight space, unhappy to cover her freshly stolen clothes in sludge.

The guards took turns stabbing through the floorboards, forcing Bylyn flat on her belly. She'd made an error, a terrible move to crawl instead of trying to run. She rolled from beneath, covered in dirt, with one chance at freedom if she tried, but she was met with the tips of seven finely honed swords.

"Get to your feet," the captain yelled.

Bylyn stumbled to stand, knowing she could not fight and that she was better at running. She spun around, hopeful she could confuse them. Her floppy dance was desperate and flailing, and a distraction while she drew the rusted blade from her corded waist and slashed at the swarming guards.

"You filthy thief." The captain rubbed his cheek and turned, a short gash visible. "You'll regret that. Take her hands," he ordered one of his men, "and while she screams, take her head."

"No, my lord," Bylyn begged. "I'm regretful. I didn't mean to cause you harm."

The guard ripped at her sleeve, pulling her wrist free and laying it across the block used to slaughter hens. Bylyn screamed as he raised the sword. Before she could blink, the blade dropped to the dirt and the guard fell with a crossbow arrow piercing his throat. She gagged at the sight of blood pouring at her feet.

The circle of guards turned their attention from the thief to whoever launched the arrow; a rider, cloaked in black, kicked their foot into the crossbow's cocking stirrup, drawing it for a second shot.

"Cut him down," the Captain of the Guard ordered, and the men raced toward the cloaked stranger. There was no hesitation as they charged the rider on foot. The second arrow flew, dropping the lead guard dead in his run as it pierced him through the eye.

The four remaining soldiers stopped.

"Who dares attack the bishop's guards? Show your face, you filthy coward," the captain ordered, but the stranger did not comply. They drew their broadsword, kicked one leg over the horse's saddle, and slipped to the ground. The blade was less than half the height of the stranger, but every swing met its target as they knocked each attacking guard to the ground.

Bylyn was captivated as she snuck toward the stranger's horse. She knew how to mount a saddle, and understood how to gallop enough to make an escape while these soldiers battled to their deaths.

"You dare to call me a coward," the stranger said, hovering over one of the few standing guards. The stranger's sword pierced the soldier's cloak, pinning him in place.

The stranger stepped back, recognizing the man. They drew the hood of their cloak around their shoulder, revealing their face.

"Captain Rasa!" the soldier said with admiration.

"Anwar Miquel, my brother." She reached to tug him to his feet. "You are looking well."

"My captain," he said. "I have missed you." He gripped her forearm for a respectful greeting. "Where have you been all these years?" As she leaned in to hug the man who was once her dedicated right hand, he fell limp against her chest.

"Oh, Captain Rasabel," the new Captain of the Guard taunted. "It appears that you've forgotten something!" He kicked at the crossbow, emptied of its last arrow.

"Bastard!" she yelled, snarling at the cowardly leader. "You'll regret this." She did not advance, but waited, anticipating exactly what would happen next.

The captain raised his sword and it crashed hard against Rasabel's own. The battering of steel against steel was not matched. This opponent was well trained, clearly having earned the right to wear the captain's insignia on his pauldron, but Rasa knew she was better.

She returned the blade strikes, one after the other, aware at the same time that the girl was trying to escape.

Distracted by the sound of her horse, she turned to watch the little thief tugging the reins in an attempt to steal her animal. She couldn't waste her strength on this man.

"Would you kill me?" she asked the Captain of the Guard.

"I would cut you into a thousand pieces and feed you to the farmer's pigs."

"And what would the bishop say?" she baited him, knowing he was no match for her skill.

"He would say 'good riddance'." Like an impatient novice, the captain lunged toward her, cocky in his attack, overextending his reach and underestimating her skills.

Rasa sidestepped easily, leaving a gap wide enough for him to fall atop the bed of amber coals. He rolled and turned in the smoldering ash, screaming like an animal being slaughtered. His guards lay scattered on the ground, dead or unable to help.

The scene was unbelievable as Rasa walked away. These soldiers were once her own. She knelt beside her once trusted friend and pulled the arrow from Anwar's back. "I am so sorry to lose you." She whispered a final farewell, grabbing the crossbow from the ground and racing toward the girl and her horse.

"Little thief," she said to Bylyn. "You'll never coax Onyx to run away with you. She is loyal to me, and me alone, now."

Bylyn did not say a word as she ran as fast as her oversized boots would allow her to move. She raced through the field, staying off the riding path Rasabel had arrived on.

"Can you outrun a horse, little thief?" Rasabel trotted beside the girl.

Bylyn didn't stop. "I can run as long as it takes for me to keep my hands and my head." She huffed.

"I promise you shall keep both." Her horse was walking easy now, capable of pacing the girl.

"You just killed the bishop's guards and bested his captain. How am I supposed to trust I'll be safe?" Bylyn stumbled, falling over the rocks hidden in the taller grass.

"You have my word that I will give you safe passage," Rasa said as she grabbed the girl by her shirt and dragged her onto the saddle.

The saddle horn dug into Bylyn's ribs. "You are a kidnapper," she screamed.

"I am no such thing." Rasa hitched a leather binding, tying the girl in place. She clicked her tongue twice and Onyx raced away from the village.

"Where are you taking me?" Bylyn grunted.

"To Acadia."

Having just escaped the dungeons of the town, Bylyn didn't want to charge off in that direction. "If you don't mind, m'lady, I would rather go away from the city of Acadia."

"But I have business there." Rasa's thighs tightened, clenching the saddle so her hands were free to hold the wriggling girl.

"Then if you'd drop me to the ground, I'll take my leave in the opposite direction." Bylyn squirmed against the saddle but could not break free from her captor's grip. "How is it possible you have the strength of many?" she asked.

"Little thief, I have spent most of my life being underestimated for my brains and especially for my brawn.

I've lived on my own for nearly two years and my body is my very best defense."

Bylyn steadied herself, gripping the woman's thigh. "So I see, and feel."

"My gear is in the forest not far from here. We'll rest Onyx and I'll pack my belongings."

"You have a camp?" Bylyn twisted so the saddle horn did not hammer her ribs. "Might you let me down and I will follow?"

"I'm not sure you can be trusted." Rasabel chuckled. "We'll get to camp and I'll make my assessment."

"I am at your mercy." Bylyn groaned. "You will show me some, won't you?"

"We will see, little thief."

"You should give me a chance," Bylyn argued. "How will you know what I can do if you don't give me a chance?"

Rasa snickered. "You make a very doubtful first impression."

The girl struggled against the restraints. "That's because you aren't seeing me at my best."

As if to offer an opinion, the horse nickered. "I will consider your release when we arrive at my camp."

It was the most Bylyn could hope for in her current situation so she did her best to enjoy not stumbling over her floppy-booted feet.

CHAPTER SEVEN

Rasabel's camp was a short ride from the inn and the confrontation left behind. She'd killed most of the bishop's guards and there would be repercussions, she knew, but she planned to address the bishop long before they would find her in the countryside.

Bylyn was eager to end the humiliating position across Rasa's saddle. This stranger had a story and some kind of history with the men they'd confronted. She also had means, with a robust horse and saddle of high-grade leather. Bylyn was ready to relax at an impressive camp, fill her belly and perhaps sneak away with something she could trade to take her from the territory.

"Will you behave if I let you down?" Rasa asked, but the girl did not answer out of stunned disbelief.

The camp was little more than a blanket of thick wool beside a ring of rocks and smoldering ash. This could not be. "What would I do?" Bylyn grunted. "There is hardly anything here."

She felt the tether loosen, no longer securing her to the saddle, and she slid from her awkward position, landing sideways in the leaf litter and grass.

It was autumn, time for the life of the forest to prepare for slumber. Cold weather was coming and she was eager to head south for warmer conditions. Night would come soon enough and she would use the cover of darkness to make an escape.

Rasabel dismounted with more grace than the little thief. "It's too dangerous for fire now. Do you know how to water a horse?" she asked.

"Is there a river nearby?" The warrior wasn't terribly smart, and Bylyn thought this would be her chance to escape. *Walk the animal to water and run.*

Rasa shook her head. "There is a basin. Take her to it." She pointed at the pit in the rocks lined with animal skin. The horse resisted the thief's tug on the reins. "Go with her, Onyx. She'll take care of you."

"Yes, Onyx. I'll take very good care of you."

Bylyn led the horse to the strange watering hole but the animal would not drink. "I don't think your horse likes me. How do I get her to do what I want?"

Rasa folded the bedding, rolling it tight so she could tie it to her saddle. "She's not one to follow if you give her latitude." She chuckled. "Tell her, don't ask."

Bylyn frowned. "That sounds very much like the way a man treats a woman." The horse tugged hard on the lead, nearly tossing Bylyn to the ground.

"I would never let any man treat me as lesser because I am a woman." Rasabel kicked the coals apart, smothering what was left of her fire. "And you should not either."

Bylyn stepped away from the horse, intrigued by the way this brute of a woman would dismiss the controlling tendencies of a man. "How is it you answer to no man and that you ride alone without fear? And why did that guard call you captain?"

Rasa leaned against the tree. This girl appeared clever for her age, and not at all afraid to speak each and every one of her thoughts. If she was to lead Rasa back to Acadia, perhaps sharing a bit of the past would build up trust. "I was once bound by the code of the bishop's guards. I trained them for more than ten years and I led hundreds of skilled fighters into battle for our mighty and holy leader."

Captivated by the warrior's bewitching dark eyes, Bylyn abandoned the watering chore and slid to the ground beside Rasa. "I'm sure our lord appreciated the sacrifice."

The woman seemed lost for a moment, disappearing in a memory. "It wasn't the bishop's approval that I wanted, nor the lord's. At least not a lord most pray to."

Bylyn was curious about the way this captain's voice softened and she wondered if Rasa worshiped a soulmate. "What was his name?"

Rasa frowned.

"It was a lover, am I right?" Bylyn asked. "You wanted his approval?"

Rasa turned to the sky, watching a bird circling beyond the treetops. "There was no 'he' in my search for approval." Her expression was hard to read; love, for sure, but also deep sorrow attached to it.

"Oh?" Bylyn was confused.

"*Her* name was Isolde." The transformation from warrior to lovestruck admirer was palpable. This 'her' in Rasa's past was more than a casual tryst.

"Her name?" Bylyn questioned, understanding that two women together was sacred to the old gods. "Blessed by the goddess, you're cherished."

"You follow the ways of the goddess?" Rasabel chuckled. "Little thief, I don't believe you."

"I swear on the flame of the Great Mother." Bylyn held her palm to her breast, mimicking a gesture the countryside covens made to honor the mother of all creation.

"The Great Mother, you say?" Rasa was skeptical.

"I promise, there is not a single goddess I won't pray to." Bylyn knelt in reverence and returned to sit. "They are the only reason I survived the dungeons of Acadia and why I cannot go back."

Rasa was as wise as she was strong, and although she could see through the lies, she also saw the terrifying truth behind them. This girl had no one and nothing. "Tell me your name, little thief."

The girl hesitated. Giving this information could damn her to the dungeons. If she hadn't witnessed the guards attack Rasa, she might have thought the former captain would return her for whatever bounty was soon to come. She needed to build trust if she wanted to escape with her head and the rest of her body.

"I am Bylyn of the Misty Shores." It was the first truth she'd told. "You've probably never heard of the place and I haven't been there since childhood."

Rasa raised her eyebrow. "I have heard and seen. It isn't a safe place for women or girls to be alone."

"Which is why you find me here in the Acadia territory."

A loud bird's call echoed close to them in the trees. Rasa held her leather-wrapped arm to the sky, made an answering bird caw, and moments later a red-feathered hawk sailed inches from the ground to land on Rasa's arm. The animal sidestepped, its wings flipping for balance until its tethering strands fell between Rasabel's fingers.

Bylyn thought this situation had gone from strange to stranger, and she didn't want to stay in the unusual situation. "You have a hunting hawk?"

"I do." Rasa smiled. "And the hawk has me."

Bylyn stood, perplexed by the odd happenings around her. "I see that you are fine here with your giant black horse and your flying companion. If it pleases you, I think I will be on my way. It doesn't look like our traveling needs are compatible." She turned, stumbling in her oversized boots as she clomped in the opposite direction of the awaiting dungeons.

Before Bylyn could leave the safety of their camp circle, Rasabel's arrow flew by her ear, landing feet from her face to lodge in the tree.

"We will travel back to Acadia together, Bylyn the thief of Misty Shores." Rasa stood, the bow light in her hand, her stance more persuasive than her words. "You have escaped an inescapable stronghold and I need you to lead me back the way you came."

"M'lady…" Bylyn shook her head. "Captain Rasabel." She steadied the vibrating arrow shaft.

Rasa frowned, disapproving the use of a former and formal title.

"I cannot take you back to Acadia," Bylyn explained. Her finger traced the fletching, running the length of the dark feather down the wooden shaft and stopping where the hammered point sank into the trunk. "If I return now, the executioner will murder me ten times over. As you've already said. I have escaped the inescapable and they must kill me, publicly, gruesomely, to save face." She attempted to remove the arrow but it did not budge.

"Only if they catch you." Rasa stretched her arm to set the bow on her horse's saddle. "And as long as we travel together, you will not be caught." She smiled, the confidence in that expression convincing Bylyn to almost believe it true. Rasa grasped the arrow and with little effort removed it from the tree.

"From the looks of the fight you had with the bishop's guards, they'll want your head, too," Bylyn argued. "Why is it so important for you to return to Acadia? What business would you have as their former captain?"

"I have one goal," Rasa rasped as she fingered the feathers on the arrow. "Business, as you say, that must be finished, and then I will take you to your freedom."

"And what might that goal be?"

Rasa wiped the bark from the arrow's point before returning it to the quiver on her saddle. She tapped the pummel of her sword. "I have only a single goal and that is to bury this blade in the heart of the Bishop of Acadia."

Bylyn stepped away, wanting to run but knowing an arrow awaited her back if she did. Laughing nervously, she questioned, "In the bishop?"

"Yes, as I said."

It was clear to Bylyn that she'd traded one lion's den for another. This warrior was surely mad and impossibly misguided if she believed Bylyn would take them to their deaths. "And you are relying on me to help you bury your sword?" She swallowed hard at the thought of this cruel Bishop's ability to reach the unreachable and make people disappear.

"You have escaped from a place no one does," Rasa said. "That is a sign from our goddess"—she leaned forward, her body tensed—"and I believe in the goddess's directives."

"It is no directive. It was dumb luck that I picked a lock and fell in a river of waste and I can't even swim."

Rasa steadied her horse. "There is time to make a proper plan."

"A plan beyond your sword meeting the Bishop's heart?"

"Precisely." Rasa kicked herself onto the saddle. "Can you ride?" She held a hand for the girl to grab.

Bylyn shook her head. She could ride, but if she planned to escape this warrior's madness she could not do it on the back of that massive animal.

"I will walk," Bylyn said. "If it pleases you."

"Walking will slow us down." Rasa snapped her hand, more insistent that the girl take it.

"I will run."

Rasa looked at the boots Bylyn wore. "You'll do no running in those."

Bylyn held her hand over her heart. "I swear I will keep up, plus that saddle is not made for two riders."

Rasa chuckled, remembering so long ago, how two fit cozily on this saddle for more than a traveling ride…

"Is this how you woo all your women?" Isolde whispered, knowing exactly how her woman's body would react.

Rasa felt the tightening of Isolde's arm around her waist and the tickle of the breathy question in her ear. "You ask as if there have been many women to woo."

"I am sitting behind you with a comfortably saddled horse following us," she teased. "You have interesting ways, Captain, wooing or not."

"I have a plan, as any good captain would. You see that horse is our second, in the event my Onyx falls lame."

Isolde laughed. "Your horse is as constant as you and the setting sun. This tale of two horses tells more about your intentions."

"My intentions," Rasa hummed. "You know my intentions."

Isolde's hand trailed across leather armor, down to the tight lacing at her hip. It was a challenge to breach the captain's protection but when she did, Rasabel reacted as she wished. "Perhaps I have intentions as well." She separated layers of linen to find her bare skin.

"Isolde," Rasa rasped. "You mustn't —"

"Oh, but I must."

Rasa cleared her throat. This memory all she had of better times that she didn't want to share with another. She withdrew her hand. "I will set a slow pace for now."

"Thank you." Bylyn chased the rider, boots flopping with every step. She was determined to get to their next camp and find a way to freedom when the warrior slept. It was a good plan, and maybe if her luck continued, she'd silence the noise in her belly too.

CHAPTER EIGHT

Bylyn wasn't sure she'd ever spent hours with such a stoic person. There was little conversation as she walked behind the mysterious warrior, who was dressed head to toe in fading black. Rasabel—what a curious name for the woman striding alongside a towering horse, carrying everything she owned in the heavy leather bags on her saddle.

As much as she wanted to satisfy her curiosity about her savior, Bylyn also wanted her freedom. More specifically, she wanted to get as far away from the executioner's blade as her rotten boots could take her.

They traveled for hours, Rasa leading the riderless horse while Bylyn collected tinder and sticks to make fire when they stopped.

Rasa broke from their path, spun against the horse's side and righted herself with a bow and arrow in her hands. The movement was like a dance as she nocked the arrow, effortlessly smooth in a way that caught Bylyn off guard.

"Move behind me," Rasa said, her bowstring taut to her cheek.

Bylyn watched the arrow fly, hitting the target of a rabbit, before she could react to the command. *The warrior is truly a skilled hunter,* she thought. *Not a fluke and also not favorable if I want to escape.*

Rasabel slid the bow into the flap on her saddle. "Do you know how to dress an animal?" she asked.

"I've lived on my own for years." Bylyn shook the loose fabric of her shirt. "Just because I was at an inn when you found me doesn't mean I carried the coin to eat there."

The warrior found the girl's need to fill the quiet with the sound of her voice annoying, as questions were never answered. "Is that a yes?" Rasa pulled the arrow from the animal and wiped the tip clean in the grass.

"Yes, I can dress a rabbit," Bylyn huffed.

"Good." Rasa tossed the animal to the girl. "Take it to the river and clean it up."

Bylyn stared at the dead thing lying in the dirt by her boots. "And what will you do while I'm dressing your kill?"

"I'll finish collecting wood for a fire." Rasa pulled a dagger from her hip and handed it to Bylyn. "Give me your tinder."

Toe to toe, Rasa towered over Bylyn by almost her head and shoulders and she felt the intimidation Rasa intended. Bylyn had few choices as she rolled the dry stick bundles out of the fold in her shirt and gave them to Rasa. Bylyn sensed she could not escape at this particular moment, but her head was loud with ways to elude her latest captor.

But there was also a fresh rabbit, a dead one, that would surely satisfy her agonizing hunger. As tempting as it was to run, her stomach was noisy, days empty, and she knew given minutes by the fire she'd eat the entire animal, entrails and all.

"I'll collect wood." Bylyn mocked Rasa's words as she kicked out of the boots. "Maybe I'll take this rabbit and run." She dropped the animal near the river's edge so she could roll the pants above her knees. She was tired of being wet and definitely tired of being told what to do.

The river water was cold but so clear she could see the fish swimming in the shallows. "I like fish," she said as she used the sharp edge of Rasa's small blade to slice through the animal's skin and belly. "I'm so hungry I could eat you all by myself." There was no emotion connected to the process as she cleaned the animal and tossed the guts in the river. She cut a branch from a tree and skewered the carcass for roasting. It wasn't her best dressed rabbit, but it would do.

"Good enough for me," Bylyn joked, balancing the meat skewer as she put her boots back on. When she returned to Rasa, everything they needed for a night in the woods was set up on the ground—everything but the fire Rasa was meant to create.

"Have you ever built a discreet fire?" Rasa asked.

Bylyn snickered. "I have made fires for many occasions, my lady."

Rasa shook her head, displeased by the girl's inability to give a proper answer. It had been many years since anyone addressed her so formally, and it didn't sound right to her ears. "I'm no lady, little thief. Call me Rasa."

"Yes, my la—" Bylyn paused. "Yes, Rasa. I have many talents, most of which have kept me alive, and building a fire no one can see is something I do well."

"Night is coming and I will leave you." Rasa held a finger up, stopping the little thief from interrupting. "While you are here, sleep lightly and I'll do the same while I'm out there."

"I don't understand," Bylyn said as she kicked the leaves into a pile for sleeping.

"I hunt at night, so keep watch for anyone who might be prowling about."

"Do you sleep?" Bylyn was put off by this woman. Her demands were high and void of gratitude or logical explanation.

"I will sleep when I return later tonight."

Rasa laid her bow across the tree limb and Bylyn found it curious that she would go night hunting without her weapons. Perhaps she was hunting something else. "Do you tryst in the woods, my la—, Rasa?"

Rasa chuckled. "There are no trysts in my future, little thief. Only the hunt for retribution. Stay close to your fire and you'll be safe. Keep watch." She unbuckled the leather strap of her saddle bag before removing it from her horse. "I'd like to trust you"—she dropped the saddle on the ground, followed quickly by the bit and reins—"but you've yet to prove your allegiance." She looped the cord of a sling around Bylyn's wrists and bound the length beneath the saddle using a tying method Bylyn had never seen.

The girl had only enough length to cook and eat, but not much more.

"In the morning, we will discuss your release once you've shown me how you escaped Acadia."

"Rasa, you would tie me up and leave me to the animals of the night forest?"

Rasabel did not answer as she unclasped her cloak, folded it neatly and set it atop the saddle. "In case someone needs to be warm."

"But the wolves," Bylyn squeaked. "And the other animals that eat small people like me?"

"I promise, I'll be close enough to protect you from the wild night creatures." Rasa disappeared into the trees, the last of the day's light marking a path.

"You promise," Bylyn mocked. She struck the flint stones to spark the tinder beneath the bundled sticks. "I could burn this rope," she said as she rested the skewered rabbit over the fire. "As if I'd run off and leave all of her possessions in the forest."

Bylyn had spent most of her life alone, traveling by the discretion moonlight created. Her thieving ways gave her no safe place to call home and she found comfort in the light of the moon. "We made a good pit for the fire," she said to no one as she rotated the skewer of meat. Her belly ached and she was tempted to steal a bit of the almost-cooked rabbit.

The snap of twigs drew her attention away from the fire. "Rasa," she whispered into the shadows. The empty scabbard lay on the ground beside the saddle. "Bound and unarmed. You would have me die like that rabbit." She heard something move through the thicket of briars. *This night is wrong*, she thought. "Wouldn't it be fitting to survive escaping the dungeons and its guards, only to die alone, tied to a warrior's saddle?"

Whispers were returned. "Death will not find you." The hushed voice was heart-stopping, musical like a song only angels could sing. Onyx stomped her feet as she followed the sound.

"Show yourself." Bylyn stumbled to stand, the rope length too short for her to appear menacing.

A woman stepped from the cover of the trees. "I am unarmed," she said, waving her hands as proof.

Bylyn steadied herself against the hypnotic sound of her voice. The woman's long hair hung past her shoulders. Her body was pale compared to the light of the night sky, but the most curious part was Bylyn's ability to look upon her in the flesh. "Yes." She swallowed hard. "You are indeed unarmed but you are unclothed as well, m'lady."

The woman looked down at herself, her body aglow under the unobstructed moon. She combed her fingers through her hair, tangled from her scurry through the trees, her smirk almost as enchanting as her voice. "Yes, I suppose I am quite unclothed." She stepped toward the saddle as if it were her own.

"It is my duty to protect those things," Bylyn said, but she could not actually move to protect them.

The stranger unfolded Rasa's cloak, pausing, her eyes closed as she held the fabric to her face.

Who is this stranger, Bylyn questioned internally, *and why does she behave with ease at the captain's clothes like she's done this before?*

The woman wrapped the dark cloak around her and the corded bottom rested on the ground, making her a few inches shorter than Rasabel.

"How do you come to be here in the forest, and without clothes?" Bylyn asked.

The woman smiled as she stepped toward the fire. "That is a story for another time," she said. "How is it you are here, among this saddle and gear?" She studied the girl, finally noticing the intricately tied rope around her wrists. "And bound to it no less with a very special cord." She had many questions as she studied the binding. This girl must be important to hold.

Spinning the best story she could, Bylyn attempted to talk her way to freedom. "I travel alone, m'lady."

"I am not your lady, girl." The woman warmed her hands near the flame, pausing to rotate the roasting rabbit. "Call me Isolde." She turned, with eyes the color of a cloudy sky.

"Isolde," Bylyn repeated. Perhaps it was the firelight that made Isolde's eyes so enchanting, or the thought of her nakedness beneath the cloak. She stammered out a response. "A beautiful name for an exquisite woman."

"Flattery." Isolde snickered. "That's adorable but it will not work on me." She focused on the roasting meat. "Tell me your name."

Distracted by the nearness of such beauty she fought to remember her name. "I'm…"

"You are?" Isolde repeated. "You have a name, don't you?"

The thief did have a name, but she also didn't know this naked lady in the woods. But then again, she was a naked lady in the woods. She couldn't possibly use nakedness as a ruse for finding the escaped prisoner of Acadia. Taking a chance, she said, "I am Bylyn of the Misty Shores."

The woman smiled and Bylyn was doubly smitten. Perhaps she could turn this to her advantage and persuade Isolde to free her. She could run, use the cover of night to put distance between whatever was happening here. Rasa would never know.

Stay or run; she struggled with the choice, remembering freedom was hers if she could convince Isolde to cut her tether. But the woman's nakedness was curious. Bylyn wanted to stay a little longer to find answers.

"I was captured by a group of thieves," she lied. "Just before you arrived they surrounded me and chased the owner of this horse into the woods. They bound me, and as long as I'm tied I can't go after her to help."

Isolde was skeptical, believing every word Bylyn spoke to be a lie. She knew this horse and its owner like she knew herself. "And if I cut you free, will you go and rescue her?"

"On my honor." Bylyn made an awkward circling gesture over her heart. Perhaps she meant it as a sacred vow, but it looked more like a fight against pesky dung heap flies. Bylyn knew little about things that were sacred, and even less about faith and higher powers, but she could pretend enough for a taste of freedom.

Skepticism in her tone, Isolde asked, "And you swear you have this honor?"

Bylyn nodded.

"And you swear the lady of this cloak did not want to keep you here for another reason."

"On my honor." Bylyn 'fought the flies' with the peculiar gesture again.

"Yes, yes—honor," Isolde mocked as she searched inside the saddle bag. "I know it is here," she whispered as she found the small but empty pouch.

"You know this soldier?" Bylyn asked. "The sullied captain of the bishop's guard."

Isolde would not cut this tether, because it was her cherished sling. The loops around the girl's wrists were better than links of chain. She knew the tying technique well. Rasa's hands had fastened this girl in place and for a brief moment Isolde thought untying the girl was a mistake.

"There." Isolde held the cord.

"Very good." Bylyn rubbed her wrists. "I was worried a night creature might find me."

As if commanding it to become the truth, a howl interrupted them. Isolde turned toward the sound. "Close, the wolf is almost here."

The snap of twigs sounded, and as she turned back toward the captive, Bylyn of the Misty Shores was gone. "Well that's not going to go well at all," she whispered.

"Gratitude, m'lady," Bylyn yelled as her oversized boots carried her deep into the forest.

The fire crackled and Isolde returned her attention to the charred rabbit. "At least I don't have to cook it tonight." She sighed. As she tore a chunk of meat from the skewer, a massive wolf stepped from the shadows. Lit by the glow of the waning crescent moon, the animal sniffed the air, taking note of every foreign scent.

Isolde held her hand out, waiting for the animal to join her and find its place by her side. "That little one played me." Her fingers sank into the thick fur around the black wolf's head. The animal rolled against her leg, exposing the soft skin of her belly. "I'm sure we can find her in the morning."

The strings tying the cloak at her neck dangled and the wolf nipped when Isolde bent for another bite of her rabbit dinner. "Uh uh." She held the knot. "It's cold tonight."

The animal didn't stop, tangling itself inside the length of fabric, connecting against bare skin. Isolde knew this game well. After two years they had an unspoken language under the light of the moon. She wrapped herself around the wolf, the heat of the fire and the animal's nearness keeping her warm. "Are you hungry?" Isolde tore off a piece of meat and the wolf licked it from her fingers.

"What have you been up to this night?" She grinned as she plucked sticks and stems from the fur. The animal took the next offered slice of meat with the same controlled lick. The fire crackled and the night fell silent as Isolde laid the skewer beside the flame. "I am tired tonight." She wrapped them tighter in the cloak, snuggling until she was fast asleep.

CHAPTER NINE

The Captain of the Guard rode through the heart of Acadia, pushing his horse beyond the limits of its stamina. Failure to retrieve the girl would anger the bishop, but news of Rasabel's return would most definitely spoil whatever was happening in the courtyard where the man enjoyed his daily afternoon entertainment.

The shock of seeing Rasabel in the region was a threat to many, including him and his position as captain. She was the ideal warrior, legendary among those who remained loyal to her leadership, and Fleur worried the consequences he might suffer from the bishop upon sharing the news of her return.

Fleur was filthy from the fight with Rasabel—his uniform fire singed and bloodstained after burying half his guards. The burns on his arms were smothered with the innkeeper's herbs and the wounds to his back ached where they rubbed against what was left of his tunic. These injuries grew unbearable until he thought of the pain that would soon come when he shared his failure.

"He will not be pleased," Fleur grumbled under his breath. He could hear the midday music as he rode, knowing the bishop was enjoying his women. The people of Acadia overlooked the bishop's inclination to disregard his vows. He was powerful, vengeful and a fortunate holy right hand with wicked tendencies.

Riding his horse through the courtyard and into the bishop's private sanctuary was near blasphemy, but he did it anyway. *He will not kill me,* he thought. *I am too important even with...* He should have stopped to wash and shave, to make himself presentable after a full day of chasing the escaped thief, but there wasn't time. As he entered the garden greens the musicians stopped their playful song and the dancers froze in place.

Fleur's horse nickered as he pulled hard on the reins.

The bishop focused on the filthy newcomer, a wine glass at his lips as he recognized the Captain of his Guard. He sipped the drink, expecting firm tannin notes but instead smelling his captain's arrival. His expression soured as he threw the cup across the garden, the red wine pouring across the ivory stone pathway.

"I know this could not be the Captain of the Guard who stops before me?" he spoke aloud to no one in particular, his tone snide and unforgiving in front of the stunned entertainers.

The captain's head hung, not out of reverence, as it should, but out of petrifying fear.

"How dare you enter my gardens, interrupt my festivities, reeking from the stench of…" He eyed the man. "Wherever you have been?" Wine-stained spittle flew from the bishop's mouth, leaving crimson specks on the perfect whiteness of his long linen robes.

Fleur towered over the bishop, a position inappropriate for the lesser man. "Apologies, my Lord Bishop. I come with news that could not wait." In his haste to dismount, the shredded uniform tunic caught on his saddle, adding embarrassment to the humiliation of defeat.

It was clear to any onlookers that the half-dressed dancers were about to be devoured by the 'celibate' man. "Leave us."

The dancers scurried through the archway, frightened to witness the wrath which was clear to follow. The lead musician stared, wide eyed and shaking, as the flutist pushed him to flee. Nothing good would happen to Captain Fleur in this garden today.

When only the bishop and his Captain of the Guard remained, the holy man asked, "What is this news?" The wrinkles around his lips highlighted his disapproval when Fleur moved upwind. "You have rid us of the thief, I presume?" He walked with the elegant grace of a dancer to sit on his gilded chair. In the eyes of most it looked more like a throne, and didn't true servants of a higher power need such worldly ornamentation?

It was clear the bishop lusted after many things.

Captain Fleur dropped to one knee, preparing for the reprimand of the bishop's staff. "I regret to share that the thief runs free." Fleur did not have time to deflect the strike to his face. He could taste the elemental flavor of blood but he dared not spit it out.

"You have failed me and here you arrive reeking of the countryside?" The bishop dabbed his spit with a flowery handkerchief from his sleeve. "I will make you her cellmate—"

With blood dripping from his mouth, the Captain interrupted, "Rasabel has returned, my lord."

The bishop's eyes grew wide, lips turned down, as the reality of the message became clear.

Fleur didn't dare look up, afraid of what he might see in the man's dark eyes. "Did you hear me, Lord Bishop?"

The leader of the church remembered the former captain and the first time she questioned his authority…

> "My lord," Rasabel said to the bishop. "I have nothing more to teach Isolde. She is incredibly gifted, so much so that she could be my second in the field."
>
> It was this captain's size he hated— her towering stature and commanding posture. Whether knowing or unknowing, the captain never lowered herself to him. She needed to learn her place in his palace.
>
> "Isolde is promised to be more than that," the bishop said. "She and I will be here at the palace, caring for the land and its people, and we will do it together."
>
> "But your vow to the church," Rasa questioned. "You cannot serve both."

"There are ways to make it so." He raised a dismissive hand. "Is there anything else, Captain Rasabel?"

"No, Lord Bishop."

"Then I dare say you should know your place… and stay there."

But there was so much more between him and the sullied captain. More lies, more betrayals and one curse that would tear at the bond between Isolde Mondurey and her Captain of the Guard. The bishop slammed his staff hard against the tile on the floor, cracking the slab into fragmented ruin. It was outrageous to believe the former captain would return to the region. It was even more impossible to think that Fleur would let her live.

"Did she attack your men?" the bishop asked.

"She killed four." Fleur swiped at the bloody slash on his face. "She and her thief gave me this."

"Weakness." The bishop stabbed the ground again. "Unforgivable weakness."

"Yes, my lord." Fleur cowered.

"So they are partners, Rasabel and the thief who escaped your duty?" His face puckered with disgust.

As Fleur expected, it fell on his shoulders: the escape, the chase and now somehow Rasabel's return. "It would appear they are traveling together." He did not move, waiting for the pain that would come from this news.

"Send out the best of my guards." The bishop eyed his captain. "If you can manage the strength to raise your sword, lead every able-bodied fighter to find them and bring their heads to me!"

"My lord?" Fleur didn't try to hide his shock. The bishop had rarely ordered such a blatant murder of one they'd called their own. Even if the entire town believed Rasabel had betrayed the mighty above, he wasn't certain they'd want her dead.

The bishop ignored Fleur's questioning words. "She travels with a hawk." He thought of the bird—how it would survive without care.

"A hawk, my lord?"

"Did you see the bird?" he asked. His cheeks flushed and his glare softened as desperation blunted the ferocity of his hatred.

Fleur shook his head. In all the chaos of fighting he could not remember such a creature.

"The hawk belongs to Rasabel." The bishop's eyes closed, not wanting to say his next words, somehow believing it wasn't still true. "The two... they are... never apart."

This commentary was confusing, but Fleur did not dare interrupt. As the bishop stood, towering over the trembling man, he explained, "She is an unusual bird with feathers as red as a lover's lips." He regretted the vows of celibacy he'd taken, remembering the moment Isolde arrived in Acadia...

"Isolde of Mondurey, Lord Bishop,"
Rasabel introduced.

Isolde did not bow or curtsy to the religious leader even though he held power over her present and future.

"You are lovely, Isolde," the bishop said as he circled around. She was more than he'd expected; a length of hair golden from the sunlight, fine skin he trembled to touch, plump lips he imagined against his own. Lovely was a modest word to describe what she was and what that did to him.

Isolde looked into his eyes as he addressed her and the Bishop stopped, struck by the color and the curious glare. He coughed. "You will find Acadia to be very accommodating to your needs." He waved around the open courtyard adorned with flowering shrubbery, fruit-filled trees and a station of musicians creating a perfect atmosphere that was far from penitent.

"Thank you, Lord Bishop," she said.

Her 'thank you' felt like a caress, like an open invitation to have her as he pleased. It was all he wanted from that moment. She was what he desired, and he was never denied.

His attempts to capture the girl's attention were dismissed that day and every day that followed, and he watched the former Captain of the Guard fall in love with his obsession. As humiliation swelled to jealousy, lust became his master.

"I did not see the bird." Fleur interrupted the memory.

The bishop pushed Fleur to the ground, his foot landing across his throat. "She is a magnificent creature with a gorgeous span of wings wider than my staff. She is… You will do everything to ensure she is not harmed. Find Rasabel and you find the bird. Bring me that traitor's head and bring me that bird." The staff pounded again, inches from Fleur's head. Pure evil had taken the holy man's soul.

"My Lord Bishop." Fleur looked up into the eyes of something he could not believe. "I will cut the animal from the sky."

The back of the bishop's hand struck hard against the captain's swollen cheek, splitting the wound wider. Blood oozed, but the man did not move.

"Rasabel can die a thousand deaths, but bring that bird to me, alive." He kicked at the man.

Fleur rolled to one knee. "It shall be done." He felt the itch of his wound and fought the urge to wipe his cheek, knowing another display of weakness would anger the bishop further. Fleur's ego could not take another scar.

"Captain, when you're done crawling around like an animal, send for the hunter Greybeck." The bishop returned to his chair.

"Yes, Lord Bishop. To hunt the hawk?"

The staff shattered the ground again. "Not for the hawk, you fool." The bishop closed his eyes, disgusted by the stupidity of his first-in-command. "Find the hunter and do it now."

Fleur scurried to his feet, looking less like a captain and more like a boy cowering from a bully. It was that way in the bishop's presence, but who could argue against the right hand of god?

Hours later, as the holy leader sat with wine and a feast for dozens to feed himself, the doors of his dining chamber rattled with a sharp knock.

They would ruin his peace. "Enter," he commanded.

"Greybeck, my lord," the guard announced and stepped out of the way. The day had been long as the palace guards avoided contact with their spiritual leader. The bishop's anger over the escaped thief seemed disproportionate to the girl's petty crimes.

"Send him in." The bishop fanned his gloved hands across his lap, leveling the single wrinkle. He was displeased that he could smell the trapper before seeing him, and his banquet of food would go to the pigs. It would take a dozen women hours in the chamber scenting with rose oils to remove the odor.

"You have called for me?" Greybeck's height was impressive; even more-so was the head of a red-pelted wolf that masked his true face. He did not kneel or place himself in a submissive manner because this holy man was not his king or spiritual leader.

The bishop scowled. "I have called for your hunting skills." He stood, a maneuver meant to position him above the hunter. "I am led to understand there is a great black wolf in the forests of Acadia and its regions."

"I have heard no such thing," the hunter said.

The bishop stepped close. "It devours women and children, whole cattle and their calves. The beast is bloodying my countryside."

"A great black wolf, you say?" Greybeck, like so many others, was interested in black wolves not only for the rarity of their pelts but also for the ferocity of their fight. The hunter thirsted for this kill.

"Larger than four or five," the bishop embellished. "It will take a man as skilled as you to find it."

"It lives in Acadia's forests?"

"Yes, and it hunts at night. Only at night." He licked his lips, which were suddenly dry from the idea of capturing the animal.

"Night is when I make my best kills." He grunted, barely keeping the bishop's attention.

"Bring it to me," the bishop commanded.

"Dead or alive?" Greybeck asked.

The bishop considered the question. How wonderful it would be to capture the animal and watch it fight for freedom. How would he keep such a secret prisoner? The idea brought a smile as he answered, "I want it alive."

"It shall be done," the hunter said, "but you will contract to pay if the animal dies during capture?"

"My payment to you is double if the animal lives."

It was a challenge, Greybeck knew. He used baited traps and spears to hunt but always to kill. With twice the normal bounty, he would figure out a way. "It will be my honor to rid Acadia of this beast."

CHAPTER TEN

Rasabel became aware of being human again, first from the stone against her rib and next from the cold breeze against her face. There were no flames in the fire pit to protect her. Naked, disoriented, and tangled in the fabric of her cloak, she remembered yesterday's encounter and her little thief.

She rolled to her knees, scrutinizing what was left of her camp. Onyx was snacking on tall grass near the edge of the trees. Her thief, Bylyn, was nowhere to be seen. The sling bundle she'd bound around the girl's wrists hung from the horn of the saddle. Rasa wondered if the girl had told a tale to escape or if she'd found the trick to untying her bindings. "This cannot be good," she whispered.

The saddle lay where she'd left it and the sword was hidden the way she had done it for nearly two years. The smell of singed meat lingered in the air and a hint of satisfaction settled as Rasabel realized her thief hadn't stolen the meal. The hawk circled the camp three times before landing on the saddle's horn.

"Did the two of you have a bit of mischief last night?" she asked the bird. The animal's head turned toward the tree line and back to Rasa. "Why don't we go find our little thief." She jumped to her feet to retrieve the clothes she'd hidden in the woods. The bundled fabric was cold against her thighs and she no longer counted the scars of survival marking her skin as she slid the shirt over her head and stepped into the trousers. Her life was a dreamless and endless cycle.

She fastened the belt around her waist. "I don't suppose you know what direction Bylyn went?" she asked the horse. The animal raised her head, chomped loudly and returned to the snack of grass. "Helpful."

The hawk had found her way to the pile of bones in the grass and picked at the remnants of charred meat. "And you?" Rasa asked. "Any clue from above?" The bird rustled its feathers before returning to the bone. "Alone in a crowd again," she jested as she hefted the saddle to the horse's back.

She studied the boot marks in the dirt around the fire pit. "If I was a little thief who'd escaped a dungeon, what way would I run?" The question needed no answer as she mounted the horse taking the trio in the opposite direction of Acadia.

~~~~~~~~~~

Bylyn felt the pain of hunger, watching from the tree line as a kitchen-hand stirred a giant pot hanging over the
~~~~~~~~~~

outdoor fire. She had chastised herself all night for fleeing from camp, and the naked woman, before sharing the roasted rabbit. She was covered in scrapes from trampling through the forest, but the cuts didn't bother her as much as the hunger. She knew she looked a mess, but hoped this woman might show pity and give her a ladle of food. She smeared a bit of dirt on her cheeks and tousled her hair a little more. If she looked like a victim instead of an escapee she might find sympathy and in turn a full belly.

Bylyn cleared her throat, careful not to scare the woman. "Spare a bit of soup, ma'am?" Bylyn asked as she approached. The grumble of her stomach was almost as loud as her request. The stewpot dangled, slung to the side away from the flame but close to the heat. It was enough to feed a large family, Bylyn supposed, and at this moment she believed she could eat like one.

"You look a fright, child." The woman led Bylyn to a chair by a table. The feathers of a chicken lay in a basket beneath, and the woman had blood on her apron from its slaughter.

Fresh chicken stew, Bylyn thought as she sat on the wobbly three-legged stool. "I'm sorry for my appearance. I was attacked by a thief in the forest on my way from Acadia. They took my horse and cart and I haven't eaten in days." Not only was Bylyn a thief but on a good day she was also a crafty liar. Unfortunately, for the last few days lies and schemes were an obstacle on her path to any and every meal.

"The warning bells sounded all day," the woman mentioned. "Perhaps it was that escaped prisoner?"

"A prisoner escaped." Bylyn did her best to sound frightened. "It could have been my attacker."

"Perhaps they took your horse to flee the region," the woman suggested.

"And my cart, ma'am." Bylyn licked her lips watching the woman ladle two scoops of stew into a gourd, and rip a chunk from a crusty loaf of bread. The loaf was a few days old, Bylyn could tell as dry bits broke away, but it would be perfect with the chicken stew.

"Have something to eat, my dear, and I'll find more appropriate clothes for you." The woman held the bowl to Bylyn.

"I'd like to keep the trousers, ma'am. It's easier to run when bandits chase me." The bowl was a hand away from her fingertips. She could already taste the stew-soaked bread.

"Bandits?" The woman pulled the bowl back, shocked at the girl's ability to escape traveling bandits. "Child, you'll need smaller boots as well, I think."

"Better-fitting boots would be lovely." Licking her lips, Bylyn reached for the bowl. "If you have a pair."

"She could also use a good paddling, too." The voice came from behind the chicken shed.

"M'lady," the woman gasped. "Why would you paddle this child?"

Rasabel dismounted. "This child is my charge. She was tasked with guarding the camp and left me in the middle of the night."

"You left me," Bylyn argued, desperate to grab the bowl, wanting the stew almost as much as her freedom.

The hawk circled the farm, eyeing the chickens in the pen. The lady of the house set the bowl on the butchering block to retrieve a sling hanging near the door. She picked a stone from the basket beneath and tucked it in the leather pocket. "Damn hawks," she said as she threaded her finger in the anchoring loop. "Got two of my hens last week."

"Please, don't do that." Rasa's gloved hand grasped the braided cord. "If you let me take my charge, we will leave you in peace. That damn hawk belongs with me."

The woman's arms dropped to her side. "Go with her, child."

"Can I still have the boots?" Bylyn's expression was hopeful as she added, "And the stew?"

The woman snatched the bowl along with the broth-soaked piece of bread Bylyn held inches from her mouth. "Liars don't get rewards from me."

Bylyn stared at her empty hand. Her stomach's growl caught Rasabel's attention but the warrior was unsympathetic. She'd hunted the day before, caught a plump rabbit and left a belly-filling meal for the girl.

"Your dinner burned to a crisp last night," she said as they walked over the hill with Onyx following close behind.

Bylyn stumbled over the rocky terrain. "You did not see what I saw last night."

"I was hunting," Rasa said.

Bylyn did not believe her. No one hunted without weapons. Perhaps the tryst Rasa was looking for had stumbled into camp and found Bylyn instead? "While you were hunting, a naked lady scared me half to death."

"A naked lady?" Rasa grabbed the thief by the shoulders. "What naked lady?"

"She came out of nowhere and made herself cozy. She even took your cloak." Bylyn touched the intricate stitching on the fabric hanging from Rasa's shoulders. Her brow scrunched with confusion. "You got it back?"

Rasabel dragged Bylyn away from the stony trail, toward the hillside where no one could watch them. "You saw a woman?"

Bylyn nodded. "I talked to her, too." She dug the crumbs of bread from her short fingernails, more than curious about Rasa'a unusual reaction.

"What did this woman say?" Rasa was dizzy from the possibility of Bylyn talking to her.

Bylyn squeezed her shirt where it covered her heart. "She said death would not find me. And the way she spoke…" Bylyn was obviously smitten. "The way her voice broke through the night…" She was animated, mimicking an arrow to the heart and pretending to fall over dead. "Her words alone nearly killed me where I sat."

Rasa steadied herself against her horse, remembering the sound…

"You think I've never held a sword before?" Isolde, frustrated with her teacher's lesson, unbuckled the chinstrap of the helmet she wore and tossed it to the ground.

"I've witnessed you with a sword. And so far, you're a good fighter." Rasa adjusted her chest plate. After a few short days together, she was learning how the woman moved. Paying attention to strengths always revealed weaknesses, and Isolde had a few. Rasa noticed how her wrist drooped when they fought left-handed, how her right leg hitched before an advance.

Where Rasa was wide, Isolde was narrow. When Isolde advanced, Rasa stood her ground. It was a perfect dance of combat but the Captain of the Guard did not know how to fight the curious attraction raging in her heart. The language of Isolde's body said many things, most of which a trained aggressor would take advantage of. Rasa picked up her helmet, determined to train her so no one would ever take satisfaction from such weakness.

"Do you know why you're here?" Isolde asked.

Rasa snickered. "I'm here because you think you're better than anyone in Mondurey." She wiped the dirt from the helmet.

"There is no one as skilled as I am," Isolde boasted.

"Very humble," Rasa teased. "Perhaps no one in Mondurey," she said, popping the helmet back on Isolde's head.

Isolde raised her sword, responding exactly as Rasa expected. She scrutinized the warrior, tipping her blade up and down Rasa's body. It was obvious by the smirk on Isolde's face that she liked what she saw in the woman, and the warrior did not shy away. "Perhaps I have a few hidden skills that make my opponents weak," Isolde goaded, her voice low and sensual, and meant to make the strong feel vulnerable.

Rasa stepped closer, raising her hand to Isolde's face. "Perhaps you do. You are skillful in many ways, of that I am certain." She fastened the helmet chin strap and Isolde gasped, obviously expecting a different move. "You are unlike any woman I've come face-to-face with in training or anywhere else."

"So what I said was right." Isolde's voice was breathy, softer, distinctly different to their fighting positions.

"I was brought here to prove you wrong." Rasa grew serious. "So that is what I will do."

Isolde invaded Rasa's carefully intended personal space, and with a tone that made the warrior weak in the knees, she said, "I look forward to showing you everything I have."

Rasa sighed, clinging to the memory. It was all she had of her beloved now. "The voice of an angel," she whispered loud enough for Bylyn to hear.

"Yes, if angels thought to visit a person like me," Bylyn said. "If I was ever blessed to have a beautiful woman, I would want her to be the one."

"What else did this beautiful woman say?" Rasa asked, desperate for anything that might reconnect them.

Bylyn chuckled. "She said she wasn't a lady. I thought that might be true since she was out in the night, naked as a newborn babe."

"She never liked the title of lady," Rasa whispered, mostly to herself. She missed so much of what her lover had been. Nurturing hands with the gentlest of touch. Passionate in the light of day and more in the dark of night. With a single glance, she could cut through the icy facade Rasa created. The warrior grabbed Bylyn's shoulder. "And her eyes, girl? Did you look into her eyes?"

Bylyn nodded. "Like the moon and the stars found shelter inside. I've never seen any like them. And when she looked at me, I felt something I cannot describe."

"Oh, yes." Rasabel sank to the ground, unable to fight the tears. "I have missed everything behind those eyes."

They sat in the open field for a long moment, waiting for the battle-worn woman to find her wits. Bylyn didn't understand the connection between the naked stranger and the person huddled on the ground.

The hawk circled three times before landing on the toe of Rasa's boot. The bird squawked, demanding attention as it hopped into her lap. Bylyn was confused as the wild creature seemed to be so much more than a hunter's trained guide.

"What I wouldn't give," Rasa said, stroking the bird's head feathers over and over, disappearing into the moment.

Bylyn felt connected to this curious warrior, invested in her from this confusing encounter. She could hear the rage of the river that had rescued her from death and desperately wanted to escape the discomfort of the moment. "I'll take Onyx for water." She tugged the lead rope.

The horse stood, locked in a defensive position, set solidly on not leaving her rider. Rasabel's focus never left the bird in her lap.

"My lad—Rasa, let me take Onyx to the river and I'll give you a few minutes to rest."

The bird startled, snapping into the sky and squawking wildly, and before Bylyn could turn toward the sound, four soldiers slid from their horses.

Rasa was on her feet, three steps from her sword, head pivoting to follow the action. Bylyn watched as Rasa pitched back to deflect a sword's killing blow. She moved with grace and power Bylyn had never witnessed in battle, perhaps because she was a coward and ran from most fights.

Bylyn stumbled behind a tree, entranced as one by one Rasa bested her attackers. The emblems on their tunics stood out; they were back—the Bishop's guards were here to take her back.

"Get the thief," Captain Fleur commanded. Bylyn positioned herself between the soldiers and the giant wall-like presence of Onyx. If she could get on the saddle, she could ride away from the fight and find safety.

A crossbow bolt whizzed by her hip and Bylyn dove to the ground. Without a sword or weapon for defense, she crawled on her belly through the grassy terrain inching back to Onyx and a hopeful escape.

Rasa deflected the blade strike of an overzealous guard, but could not prevent a crossbow bolt from penetrating her thigh. Her sword fell to the ground and Captain Fleur was there. His fisted sword hand struck hard and Rasa took the blow to her face, seeing lights dance behind her eyes.

Why am I fighting to save this thief? she thought as the captain ripped the crossbow bolt from her body. The arrow's exit was more painful than its entry and the sound of her scream brought the guard's pursuit of Bylyn to a halt.

The pain was a reminder, reaffirming why she fought. "Bastard!" Rasa's fingers curled around her sword handle into a fist. The uppercut met Fleur's chin with all her focused strength, dislodging the helmet from his head. The force of their entanglement tumbled the two against the soldier aiming to fire his crossbow at Bylyn.

The weapon tipped as the man fell, launching the bolt into the air. The unintended target squealed as it spiraled to the ground.

"No!" Rasabel yelled.

"Not the hawk!" Fleur struck the archer with the hilt of his sword, knocking him unconscious. "Not the hawk!" *There would be consequences*, he thought as he watched the animal hit the grass.

They stood face to face, the old captain against the new.

There were no thoughts left as Rasa's rage and training took control. The first swing was meant to kill as her muscles absorbed the contact.

Fleur deflected but the handle's vibration rattled through his body, nearly causing him to lose grip on his sword.

Rasa could not see the world around her as her second swing struck with crippling strength.

Fleur stumbled, fighting to stay on his feet as he lost feeling in his arms. These were advances he did not understand, a strength of three soldiers crashing on him by this solitary warrior.

Fueled by two long years of emotion, Rasa did not show mercy. Her attack was relentless as she struck the man to the ground, out of her mind, huffing to catch her breath as the tip of her sword lingered over his chest.

"Kill me." He loosened his breastplate, revealing his bare skin. "If you don't do it, the bishop will."

Rasa clenched his tunic, her knuckles white with rage. "You." She shook him, before tossing him to the dirt. "Suffer with what you've done," she said, savoring the thought of Fleur's death at the hands of that heartless holy monster. "If he doesn't kill you, I will come and do it myself." She struck the captain's temple with the pommel of her sword, dropping him like a stone.

Rasa turned, checking her surroundings, and saw only one petrified soldier left standing. The captain had arrived with three and all but one lay lifeless in the grass. Her sword dripped with blood as she approached the last man.

"Don't kill me, m'lady." His voice wavered and his body trembled, shivering like it was cold but reeking of fear. The tunic draping his armor was clean of battle stains.

A child, she thought. Rasabel removed his helmet. "You're only a boy."

"I'm eighteen."

"Do you know the bishop of Acadia?" she asked.

He nodded.

"Take the captain's horse and tell the bishop that Rasabel of Gladeview is coming for him."

He staggered, unsteady on his feet, desperate to escape, hoping an arrow would not find his back as he rode away. He kicked a boot into the stirrup and the frightened horse spun as the boy balanced himself on the saddle.

"Go now!" She slapped the horse's flank, driving the animal toward the town of Acadia.

Rasa scrambled across the field to where the hawk lay. A single arrow was lodged in its breast, hooking the wing through the other side. "Get my horse," she screamed at Bylyn.

It was mystifying how the mare knew and let Bylyn lead it to Rasa. "There is a dagger in your saddle bag," Bylyn said. "Shall I use it? We should not let it suffer."

Rasabel's hands twisted the fabric of the thief's shirt. "You cannot kill this bird." She pushed the girl away. "If she dies, I have no reason to live." Rasa rummaged through her saddle bag, removing the panel of fabric wrapped around a fine linen bundle. The bird squealed and squawked as she swaddled it tight to immobilize it.

"Take her." Rasa pushed the thief toward the horse. "Take her now!" she yelled.

Bylyn's arms went up to refuse the bundled animal. "M'lady." She was confused. The warrior was bleeding; her hands trembled as she held the dying bird.

Rasa's force seemed otherworldly as she positioned Bylyn's free hand on the horn of the saddle and raised the floppy booted foot into the stirrup. "Get on my horse."

"I cannot ride her, m'lady," Bylyn argued. "She will not let me."

Rasa felt the sting of her thigh wound. She clutched the bloody injury and the color on her hand seemed unreal compared to injuries received before. But this was unlike any previous battle scar as the urgency of the frail animal came into focus. The hawk was small—it could not bleed like her, and without help it had no chance of survival. "Get on my horse." She raised Bylyn's body to the saddle as if the girl were light as a feather.

"Take her," Rasa screamed as she forced the bundled animal into Bylyn's arm.

Bylyn trembled, adrenaline fueling her fear. "I cannot ride without killing this bird."

"You ride toward the setting sun. Go hard and do not stop." Rasa felt the sting of her arrow wound. "Onyx will know."

"The bird will not live," Bylyn pleaded, trying to pass the bird back to the warrior.

"She must live." Rasa's tears fell. "Ride. Onyx will do as you ask. You'll find a castle in ruin and the keeper there will know how to help us."

"And if the bird does not live?" Bylyn asked.

"Then I will hunt you down and return the favor." Rasa swatted her horse's flank. "Take them to Intan, Onyx. Go!"

Bylyn steadied herself in the saddle; having spent her childhood riding on stolen horses without a saddle, she could manage Onyx's hard gallop. The direction of travel was her concern; how would the horse know? How was she supposed to keep the bird in her arms from dying, and what or who was Intan?

Rasa listened as the horse's hooves echoed until they faded away. This could not be—this was not how they should end.

Rage coursing through her body, fueling every move, she dragged Fleur into the bushes. "I should kill you for this," she said as she stripped the unconscious man down to his skin. She felt numb as she stared at his fresh burn wounds. She found nothing unpleasant about tying him to the tree, adding insult to the situation by using his own belt and tunic cords. Fleur made no sound as she left him there to face whatever was to come.

She stripped to her skin as she stumbled toward the river, relieving herself of the bloodied trousers. She felt the injury to her face as she tossed her sweat-soaked clothes into the water. Her saddle bag had more, she knew. The realization that Onyx was not here struck her heart, and the thought of failure crippled her with fear. She would not play the mind game as she watched her clothes disappear in the rapids. Perhaps she'd let go, allow the river's current to take her away along with the blood and pain. It would be so easy.

"But Isolde," she whispered.

The wound in her thigh seeped and she felt weakness like never before. "Stay awake," she reminded herself. She could not afford to lose her senses. She wished for more daylight. She wished for night to never arrive so she could make it to Intan's castle, but the setting sun would come.

She didn't want to consider what Bylyn would do if they didn't arrive in time.

"I'm with you," she cried. "Ride hard, Onyx."

She dropped to her knees on the river bank. "I'm sorry I can't take care of you." She crawled into the cold water, rolling onto her back so the icy current could cleanse her wound. "Stay near the shore," she whispered as she waited for the ripples to carry her away. It would be so easy to let it all go, to let her beast arrive in the river where it could not swim… but there was Isolde. She must not ever forget Isolde.

She did not fight. She surrendered to the sensation of icy water against her battle-weary soul. The best she could hope for now was to make it to Intan's castle before morning.

CHAPTER ELEVEN

"**I** want to have you." The breathy words were warm against her neck.

"Is," Rasa rasped. "We aren't safe in here."

Isolde unlaced the cording of Rasa's leather bodice, a restrictive shield for a battle they would not have in the armory shed. "We are safe with each other. That is all you need to know."

"Isolde." Rasa hissed her name as cool fingers danced across her ribs. She did not fight, not in earnest, as her body relaxed against Isolde's explorations.

"Yes, say my name, my love." Isolde's tongue dipped along the thick ridge of her

> *lover's abdomen, trailing a way to the sensitive scar on her hip. "I want to hear you say my name while I claim you with my mouth."*
>
> *"Oh, yes." Rasa arched, her fingers clenching at the armory wall, desperate to stay upright as her muscled legs weakened beneath her lover's tight hold. "I am yours, Isolde," she hissed, as feverish wet kisses tickled her thigh.*

It was life saving—the memory, the moment—but it wasn't real life… not any longer. Rasa opened her eyes, tears streaming down her cheeks as she realized where she was and why her thighs were wet. There was no love making, no intimate devouring of her body by the only woman she'd ever wanted to love her.

Rasabel rolled to her side, the fresh crossbow wound grinding against the pebble and sand covered riverbank. This pain was her life now. She sobbed. "Isolde." Her prune-rippled fingers dug into the frothy sand of the shoreline. "Isolde."

~~~~~~~~~~

Rasabel was right about one thing when she set Bylyn on the horse: Onyx knew where she was going and never stopped. There was something unique about the relationship between the warrior and her mare, and the more time Bylyn spent with them the less it made sense that they lived in the wild.
~~~~~~~~~~

Bylyn's legs ached from trying to stay in the saddle while cradling the bird as if her life depended on it, which, she understood from Rasa's threats, it did. The trees faded behind her as she rode through the sweeping, grassy hills. She hadn't been this far from Acadia or the neighboring regions since she was fourteen and she remembered why. There was nothing for miles—not a house, farm or village, and without people there were no pockets to pick or meals to be had, and she could use a meal, hot or otherwise.

"Don't die on me, bird," Bylyn said as the ruined buildings came into view along the horizon. "We've made it this far. Don't leave me to die at the hands of your keeper."

The path to approach the castle was smothered with overgrowth of weeds and briars. The outer walls, which once held a portcullis, were unmanned and crumbling. The secondary bridge to enter was drawn up tight, and without dismounting she reached to ring the bell in the vacant guard stand. The rope was frayed and she worried it would break when she pulled it down. A fragment of bird nest fell before the tone rang flat.

No one came. She rang the bell once more and again silence was returned. She thought about tossing the animal in the dirt, riding miles from the dying bird and the out-of-control former soldier who'd sent her on this mission.

She rang the bell one more time, willing to set her new plan in motion if no one came.

"Stop ringing that damn bell." The voice was shrill, like stray rocks grinding between a miller's stones. "What do you want from me?"

A shadowed figure was the only person Bylyn could see. "Are you Intan?" she asked, knowing he probably was, but if he wasn't, it might not end well for her or the wounded animal.

"Yes, but that is Father Intan to you." He leaned over the edge for a closer look. "Why are you bothering me? I don't have the means or the fortitude to support your need for charity."

He doesn't have manners, either, Bylyn thought. "I have a hawk here, Father," Bylyn yelled. "She is a wounded bird."

"Good hunting, m'boy," he yelled. "Bring it up and we can break bread together."

"No, sir." Bylyn cradled the animal to her chest as if the man could rip it from her arms. "We cannot eat this bird."

He grumbled, squinting as if he could get a better look from his height above. "Is it carrying a disease?"

"This bird is not sick, Father." Bylyn begged internally for the strength to share her dilemma with this half-witted man.

"If we can't eat it, then why are you bothering me about it?" he scolded, turning to leave.

"This bird is a companion, Father."

"A fighting bird. Good cheer!" He shook a celebratory fist. "Wounded in battle, I see. The meat will be tough but I'll stew it. Then we dine together. Come in, come in!"

Bylyn's eyes widened. She needed to get to the point. "No, Father Intan, this bird is the companion of Rasabel of Gladeview."

The man leaned over the wall, nearly falling to get a closer look from the second-story balcony. "Why didn't you say that from the beginning?" He scurried to the drawbridge chains. "You say she's wounded?"

"Aye, Father."

The drawbridge dropped like a stone, setting a burst of dust at Bylyn and the animals. "Bring her in. Hurry and bring her in." He made his way down the spiraling stairs to the entrance of his crumbling fortress.

Bylyn didn't have time to dismount before the man took the bird from her hands. Their face-to-face meeting was not what she expected. This holy man, married to a higher power, was more foul than a farmhand after cleaning a sty. She fanned her face to clear the stench of his breath. His unkempt clothes had the odor of a working man, but his hands were too soft for such prolonged activity. Most offensive of all was the sour aroma of bitter wine coming from his body.

He stared at Bylyn in disbelief. "You're a girl."

"I am." She shrugged. "I was born that way, Father."

"Can't have girls wandering," he mumbled. "Stable the horse behind... over there." He pointed to the shelter, not more than three hands above Onyx's height. The roof covered half the structure, which was more protection from the weather than the animal had most nights. She hesitated, her attention torn between care for the horse and watching Father Intan walk away carrying the bird she'd sworn to protect.

"I did it." She patted Onyx's shoulder. The animal raised her head, a reminder that she'd done most of the work. "Right, *we* did it."

Bylyn's mission to find Intan was complete but she needed to know that the hawk would live. Strange happenings were going on between Rasabel and this priest, and Bylyn could not make sense of them. What connection did the former Captain of the Guard share with this drunkard of a man?

She unbuckled the saddle from the mare and lifted it to rest on the rail. She didn't bother to empty the saddle bags but she noticed the sword, crossbow and bow still tethered in their places.

"She's out there alone, with a terrible wound, and unarmed," Bylyn mumbled. What would a warrior do without the weapons of war? She had to trust Rasa would be safe for the night.

Bylyn made her way to the oversized door leading inside. She was not surprised when every bit of the inside of the great entrance hall matched the outside. The old man was left to tend multiple buildings alone, and it was obvious he lacked the skills to do it.

"Hello." Bylyn wandered through the vast space listening to the echo of her call. The returning silence was sorrowful and everything about the room made her freedom feel more free. The table stood crooked, a leg balanced on a splintered log with only one of the four chairs around it unbroken. The drinking cup lacked a solid handle while the side table held a plate of rotting fruit. As hungry as she was, she didn't dare touch a piece. The life of a lonely soul was obvious, and she didn't envy it even a little. She looked up at the hole with light shining through; it was leaky, but at least he had a roof over his head.

She froze as Father Intan shuffled through the hall, mumbling a list of plants and tinctures he required. He was planning to cure the bird, and she thought it incredible. What could you do with the animal to save its wing? Who would keep a bird that did not fly? She took a chance, believing her thieving skills could help her find the animal wherever it was inside the castle. What if the priest's list of ingredients were better for making a stew, after all?

Father Intan lit a candle from the fireplace mantle and mounted it inside a lantern. "I'll be back," he said. "Rasabel was right to send her here. I know what to do. Stay away from her, now," he warned before racing from the great hall.

"Stay away?" Bylyn mumbled, mocking his threat-filled warning. "That's almost an order to investigate what you're doing, Father." She exited the hall through the same door the priest had used to enter. The light of the moon pierced the window frames, dizzying as she made her way through the shadow-bathed corridors. Each hall seemed to lead to the wrong destination, until she heard a horrifying groan. *Human, not animal*, she thought. *Curious*. She followed the sound, knocking a soft tap against each heavy wooden door she passed.

"Hello?" Silence followed the first door and she tapped two more. The corridors seemed endless. She found herself turned around. She tapped her knuckles a few times against the fourth door.

"Yes, you can come in."

Bylyn hesitated, the voice impossible. She'd heard it just the night before, coming from the naked woman in the woods. *How?* she wondered. *How could this angel's voice be here?*

"Hello," Bylyn whispered as she pushed the huge wooden door open. The hinges creaked as they moved enough for her to see inside. She blinked as if somehow it would alter this reality, but it did not.

The woman lay atop the ramshackle bed, little more than a cot thatched haphazardly together by obviously unskilled hands. This cobweb-riddled room was no place for a lady, especially one who lay naked partially covered with the linen that once bound the arrow piercing her breast. Bylyn stumbled against the door, terrified by what she saw.

"M'lady?" Bylyn asked.

The woman shook her head, unhappy being called by the title. "Isolde," she rasped.

This is impossible, Bylyn thought. "Are you a mystical spirit or are you human flesh?" she asked, afraid what the answer might be.

Isolde's head turned as she whispered, "I am neither and I am both."

"But the hawk," Bylyn said. "She was wounded." It was obvious the woman knew in what condition the bird had arrived.

"Yes," Isolde strained to answer.

Bylyn steadied herself against the wall, needing something solid to affirm she wasn't trapped in a dream.

"But how?" Isolde asked, begging for an explanation for her injuries. "How was the hawk wounded?"

"There was a terrible battle." Bylyn moved beside the bed, covering Isolde's naked body with the tattered blanket near her feet. "Rasabel fought her attackers like no one I've ever seen." Her arms flailed to demonstrate the swordplay. "She bested more than twenty of the Bishop's guards."

"Twenty?" Isolde questioned, her voice weak.

"At least." Bylyn stretched the truth, believing it would do no harm.

Isolde winced, feeling the pull of the arrow as she adjusted to follow the animated storyteller.

"Rasabel was struck by an archer's bolt… and then the hawk." Bylyn stopped.

Isolde closed her eyes, dreading the answer to her next question. "Was she badly injured?"

"The hawk?"

Isolde held the protruding arrow, her fingers bending the ribs of its fletching feathers. "Rasabel."

"Not until the Captain of the Guard tore the arrow from her thigh. She was bleeding, but I'm sure she will be fine."

Isolde whispered, "She's alive." A sigh of relief was obvious in her slowing breath. She'd thought the worst as she lay with the arrow in her breast, waking to a wound she did not understand.

"I have what we need." Intan pushed the door open, bumping against Bylyn. "What are you doing here, girl? You shouldn't be in here." He pulled the back of Bylyn's shirt until her body crossed the threshold. Before she could argue to stay, the door closed in her face.

Bylyn could not believe what her eyes had seen. The woman from Rasabel's camp, the angel who had freed her from Rasa's bindings, lay in the man's bed with an arrow in her chest. The same arrow the hawk took only a few hours earlier.

~~~~~~~~~

"I am sorry for what I have to do," Intan said as he ground the herbs in the stone mortar and pestle. "I never wanted to bring you pain… more pain," he corrected.
~~~~~~~~~

"It is not your doing, Father." Isolde was too weak to think about the situation beyond the arrow in her breast. Surviving this wound felt impossible, but the girl's visit made it clear—knowing her love had survived gave her strength to fight.

"This will not go easy." He poured water across her chest to rinse the blood and debris from the base of the arrow's puncture.

"Do what you must, Father." Isolde watched him work, pinching and whispering measures to mix the herbal salve.

"Are you ready?" he asked as he tore the last of the linen to prepare for the inevitable blood. "It will bleed, but the remedy will work better than a hot blade."

"I am ready," she whispered. The wood was warm against her ice-cold hand as she gripped the frame of the bed.

Intan did not give another warning as he clenched the arrow's shaft, adjusting his fingers for a solid hold. Isolde stared permissively, awake and aware that her life had closed in a circle around this man.

Her scream pierced the silence of the castle ruins as the arrow ripped away; blood ran, bright red in contrast to the dingy gray linen.

Intan could not manage the flow as her glassy gray eyes stared back at him. "It is a lot of blood." He dropped the soaked rag at his feet as he took another.

Isolde closed her eyes, concentrating on contracting her chest muscles. It was her only way to fight.

The priest grabbed her hand. "Hold this and push down if you have strength." He smashed a handful of herbs, working it into a ball.

In her weakened state, Isolde did what she could, but the blood ran between her fingers. She watched, feeling no longer attached to her body when he removed the bandaging and filled the wound cavity with the herbal concoction. The salve bubbled and burned, hardening the red flow into a hazy brown crust.

"Breathe," Intan reminded her.

Isolde's tears fell to the bed as she fought back every sign of weakness.

"It is not terrible," he said, but for him it would not be.

For two years Isolde experienced "terrible" on many levels. She knew how to be without the comforts of a home, how to bear the isolation of *alone* as more than a passing emotion. She knew survival like no other but one; Rasabel, the lover she could never touch or see. For Isolde, terrible had teeth baring down into her helpless soul.

She did not turn away to hide from the experience of the last hour. She knew what her eyes could do. She knew they could destroy a lover, but she also knew they could bring the unwilling to their knees. She saw it then in the priest's eyes: self-loathing smothered with fear.

It was enough for now as she thought of her beloved. She could endure anything as long as she knew her Rasabel had survived.

"I will leave you to rest." He draped the bowl of salve with a cloth and picked up the bloody linens. There was nothing else to do.

~~~~~~~~~~
~~~~~~~~~~

Bylyn sat beside the hearth, waiting for what might come and not believing what was real. Magic curses were living inside that woman, and Bylyn wanted to know how. She'd followed the maze of corridors back to the dining table. A crock bubbled over the fire in the fireplace and although it smelled as rotten as the fruit on the side table, she was hungry enough to take a chance on the old man's food.

She hooked the pot with a poker, pulling it close. She could identify a potato chunked with carrot and something brown. The single bowl on the hearth was all she needed as she plunged the dirty ladle in for a serving.

It looked terrible and smelled worse but she would eat. The wine decanter was heavy so she filled the broken mug to the top. A horrible scream echoed through the halls as she set her meal on the table.

"He must have done it." Bylyn rubbed her chest trying to imagine the pain of an arrow ripping from her own breast. She whispered to the empty room, "Professing you are neither human nor mythical creature is a very right thing to say, Isolde." There was some kind of curse here between Isolde, Rasabel and Father Intan, and once her belly was full Bylyn would coax the truth from the weary old priest.

CHAPTER TWELVE

As Intan dragged a bench across the room, the legs left a trail in the dust on the floor. Every movement he made was followed by a grunt or a groan. She sat in *his* chair, at *his* table, eating *his* soup from *his* bowl. After the strain of caring for Isolde, his patience for this stranger was terribly thin.

She was eating so quickly she could not have tasted a bite. "I see you have helped yourself to my supper," he grumbled.

"I was hungry, Father." The girl wiped her mouth on her sleeve, pausing her gobbling. "I hadn't eaten in days."

"You haven't washed in days either." He fanned a hand in front of his face.

There was something immediately familiar about the priest as he waved his hand. This man of god was a drunk, a mirror image of the one who'd abandoned her. The smell was real, the mannerisms so much the same, but her face was not sore from a beating, and there was not a bruise marking her skin. This man was exactly as she'd experienced most of them, reeking of excuses.

She pinched her nose and leaned away, hoping humor would be the only defense she'd need. "I believe that is the filthy stewpot calling the kettle charred."

He sniffed himself and shrugged. "Perhaps I am a stinky man, calling a stinky girl stinkier," he snipped.

"There is no 'perhaps' about it, Father. There are only two stinky and hungry people sitting side by side."

"Who do I have to impress?" Intan grumbled. "I am always alone." He eyed the cutlery and dish the girl used as she continued to shovel food into her mouth. Without a second bowl to eat from, he hooked the pot with the fire poker and set it on the table. His slurping was louder as he ate his meal using the serving ladle as his spoon.

It was impossible for Intan not to stare as she ate, and he wondered how the young girl came to be in his home, entangled in the complicated lives of Rasabel and Isolde.

Breaking the silence Bylyn asked, with a mouthful of potato, "I must know what you did to her in there? I heard the scream."

"Yes, girl. I suppose you did."

"I have a name, you know." She tapped the spoon toward her chest. "You could call me Bylyn instead of girl."

"Bylyn." He cleared his throat, about to say something more until she interrupted.

"Tell me she lives." Her hand trembled as she set the spoon in her bowl.

He nodded. "She lives."

"Now tell me how?"

Intan shook his head. "You would not understand."

"I know I look simple to you, Father, but I am not stupid." She set her spoon in the bowl. "I am not the child you think I am. I have seen many things in my eighteen years of life but what and who I saw in that bedchamber I cannot explain."

He huffed. "It is too tragic, Bylyn."

"So you do know?" She pushed the bowl away, more curious than ever before.

He tried to resist telling the story, bringing up a past that they had endured. Keeping the secret was part of his penance, but the girl already knew too much, and by the look in her eyes she had no intention of allowing his silence to continue.

"You must tell me, Intan," she prodded. "I brought her here. I fought beside Rasa. I think I've earned the right to know."

He turned to her with deep-set eyes, the lost stare reflecting his damaged soul. "You don't know what you're asking, girl." His face was shadowed, lit eerily by the fire in the hearth.

Bylyn was frightened by what he would share.

"It haunts me every day, and I have been a distant witness for these two years."

Bylyn wouldn't pretend any longer that forces beyond reality connected this sloppy priest with the beautiful woman in the bedchamber up the stairs. She knew what she saw. She had already pieced the truth from the bits she'd experienced, and all she wanted was the single detail connecting what her eyes could not believe they'd seen. Impatient, she blurted, "Isolde is the bird. Through some kind of curse she becomes the bird I carried to you before sunset."

Intan's head hung lower as he scooped a mouthful of food. Sensing his resistance, Bylyn pushed her mug of wine into his hand; from her experience, a cup or two would loosen his tongue.

He downed the drink with three loud gulps and Bylyn poured again. Twice more she filled the cup before the old man found the courage to speak. Drunken men were so easy.

"My dear girl, by some strange twist of fate you have fallen into a sorrowful tragedy." He emptied the cup and did not bother to wipe away the dribble that trailed from his mouth.

"So it seems," Bylyn said as she filled the mug for a fifth time. Intan consumed wine like the man who raised her.

His speech was slow, deliberately precise as he began. "She," he nodded toward the tower where Isolde lay, "is from the house of the village of Mondurey, the Lady Isolde. Although she never liked the title, she was sworn by birthright to one day marry a wealthy, suitable highborn." He dropped his ladle spoon in the pot and pushed it away. Choosing more of the drink, he continued, "Isolde came of age in a village of her family's keeping. A place known for raising strong warriors, a culture sworn to protect with skills centuries old. Isolde didn't want many things but she craved those skills, and having only an uncle as her mentor, she learned the art of combat. The young girl trained until she could best every warrior in Mondurey."

"So she knows how to use a sword as well?" Bylyn asked. Dissatisfied with the emptiness of her belly, she used Intan's ladle to scoop another serving into the bowl.

"Not only a sword. She's skilled with a dagger, a longbow, crossbow, but silent and quite deadly with a simple sling. She is gifted beyond almost all."

Bylyn caught his emphasis on the word almost. "Someone bested her?" she asked.

"Bested her, guided her, schooled her in the art of war, and eventually won her heart," he said. "Love was not something either of them could fight."

"This warrior, the one who earned her heart." Bylyn did not need to guess. "It is Rasabel, the Captain of the Guard. I know it is."

He stared at Bylyn, a gaze wrecked with fear and something more... regret. Clinging to the hope that he could escape the retelling, he asked, "So... you have met Gladeview's Rasabel?"

Bylyn shook her head. "You know I have." She tipped her chin toward the stable where Onyx rested. Anyone who knew the warrior also knew she commanded the will of that stunning mare.

"Yes, I suppose it is obvious now." He cleared his throat. "The story of their love will break your heart." He stopped. It was apparent the rest of the details were the worst part.

"Please, Father Intan." Bylyn filled his cup again. "Tell me how this curse came to be."

Head shaking, hands trembling to hold the mug, he sipped. The wine spilled over his fingers as he shared the story of Isolde and Rasabel. "As I said, when Isolde came of age, her fighting skills were beyond any in Mondurey village. Eager to stay in Isolde's good graces, hoping for more of the Mondurey riches, her uncle sent a message to the Bishop of Acadia, searching for a teacher who could advance her training." He leaned against the back of the bench, remembering what he could as his mind clouded from the wine. "My lord, the bishop, sent his best: a fearless warrior, unmatched in skill and undefeated on the battlefield. The bishop had hopes of luring the young woman to Acadia and convent life. As you know, this warrior was also the captain of the bishop's guard."

"Rasabel," she whispered, in awe of the person she'd tried to escape.

"Yes, she arrived by horse to meet her student." He chuckled, remembering Rasa's initial resistance to the assignment. "Isolde was wild in spirit and extreme in confidence, but the captain… the captain had plans. Rasa arrived in Mondurey on an animal no other could ride, but everyone took notice."

Bylyn considered the creature that had delivered her and the hawk only hours before. "It is the black horse, Onyx?"

"It is." He forced a smile. "I remember our first encounter. The pair were magnificent to see. I'm sure Isolde was excited in theory, but she and the captain did not have a pleasant first meeting."

"The captain can be—"

"Intimidating," Intan interrupted.

"Yes, that and persistent."

"At the very least." He chuckled. "Rasabel arrived a few days after the death of Isolde's uncle. The passing was sudden but the agreement to train was already set in motion."

"How is it that Isolde was not betrothed?"

He sighed, remembering the youthful spirit of the wounded woman resting upstairs. "She would never be, as she loves a woman, you see. Only ever loved women, and that is sometimes how we are born."

"They are both lovely in their own way." Bylyn blushed.

The old man glimpsed the girl's obvious admiration. "Ah, I see." Intan made the connection that this was Bylyn's way as well. "Two women being in love was never the issue," he clarified.

She leaned in as she asked, "What was?"

"The secret agreement her uncle had with the Bishop of Acadia."

"What was the agreement?" she asked.

"Upon her uncle's death, if she was not wed or betrothed, she would give herself to the church."

"But she—"

Intan interrupted. "The captain and Isolde trained for weeks before becoming friends. It took months for them to admit an attraction, and after that understanding their devotion grew until they were almost inseparable."

"They are a real love story." Bylyn's cheeks flushed.

Intan amended, "A truly tragic one."

"Tell me what happened after they fell in love."

Intan frowned. "The bishop allowed Isolde to grieve her uncle's passing. Four months passed and in that time he negotiated his plan to secure a profitable marriage or a vow to the church."

Bylyn's eyes teared. "Isolde was meant to wed… with a man?"

He nodded. "A not-so-innocent boy, selected by the bishop himself, as it would theoretically advance the bloodlines and transfer Mondurey and all its wealth to the church."

Bylyn wrinkled her nose at the thought of the angelic woman in the hands of anyone other than Rasabel. Impatiently she blurted, "But they fell in love?"

It was the first true smile Intan shared. "It was impossible to hide when you saw them together."

"What happened?" Bylyn asked. "How were they cursed?"

He pushed away from the table, pacing with the cup in his hand, spilling wine with every step. "The bishop summoned the Captain of the Guard to transport Isolde and her dowry to the palace. When he met Isolde, she became his obsession. He required daily contact to 'nurture her soul.' Isolde was polite at first, but the bishop's admiration turned into lust. He saw her training with Rasabel and knew they were more than student and teacher. He ordered the captain away from Acadia, but she refused. As leader of the guard, she'd already been away for months to teach Isolde in Mondurey. The man inside those holy robes wanted what he could not have."

"He's a bishop!" she yelled.

"Married to the lord of creation, no less," Intan added, shuffling back and forth in front of the fireplace.

"What did Isolde and Rasa do?" Bylyn asked.

"They planned to be wed in secret."

Her elbows rested on the table as she tried to follow his continued pacing. "And the bishop discovered their plan?"

His body tensed. "They were betrayed," he said. "Rasabel sought the counsel of a trusted friend, asking for a private ceremony."

"The friend betrayed them, didn't he?"

"Right after they said their promises of forever." Intan spat. "They never had a night together as wives because the weak betrayer told the bishop of their plan to flee Acadia."

"What did the bishop do?" she asked.

The old man walked out the oversized front door and Bylyn chased after him, stopping when they reached the stabled horse.

Bylyn grabbed Intan's shoulder, spinning him around to look at her. "What did the bishop do to them?"

"The bishop made a pact with the powers of hell," Intan rasped. "Placing a powerful curse on their union. Something so vile no one could ever imagine possible."

"They can never be together." She ran her hand across Onyx's back, trying to comprehend what it would be like to disappear into an unknowing creature.

"It is so much worse than that. They are women forced into living animal half-lives. Isolde soars above as the red-feathered hawk circling in the sky, and Rasabel is the wolf howling at the moon until she finds Isolde."

"I have heard the wolf. There is no chance for them when one is in the flesh while the other is an animal," Bylyn whispered.

"Yes." He tugged a pile of hay from the feed crate. "The cruelest part of it all."

"And there is no way to undo this curse?" she asked.

He huffed, wheezing from the feeding chore. "I have dreamed many times that there might be a way."

"How is that possible?" she asked, "to make dreams become the truth?"

"There would have to be an oddity, a strange celestial occurrence. I have read the sun and the stars do this. What I've uncovered is in four days there will be such a thing; a night without a day and a day without a night."

"There is no such thing," she yelled. "You are drunk now, Father. The sun sleeps when the moon shines. The two can never come together."

"That is what the Bishop thought, but what if it could be so?" He pushed away from the fence, shuffling back inside the great hall.

"Why do you know all these details? These private things?" she asked, getting dizzy from his pacing.

The man turned, ashamed to show his face, but Bylyn was very good at reading people. His part in this tragic tale was now very clear. "It was you," she accused. "You betrayed their love. You're the reason all of this is happening."

It was the part of the story that led him to drink, that led him to be in the crumbling palace—repercussions of an inexcusable choice. "This is the truth, girl."

Hate bubbled in her gut, churning the belly of food into a rancid ache. She could not believe it and yet seeing him, she knew the truth. "How could you?" She stomped, snapping the man from an abyss of self pity.

"I was weak." It was all he could say. Those three words were not an excuse but his reality. Weakness cost Isolde and Rasabel everything.

Having fought with the former captain, and rescued Isolde, Bylyn was invested in their lives. "I cannot believe Rasabel sent me to you, her betrayer."

"Yes, but who else would know the terrible role I have played and how to help the bird who is Isolde?"

"Only you." Bylyn wrinkled her nose, disgusted less by his foul stench and more by his foul soul.

"Yes, me. But now there is an opportunity to right this wrong."

"How?" Bylyn was skeptical, sensing the desperation in his words. "By making the day into night?" she mocked.

"It is serendipitous." He prodded the fire. "That wound to her breast brought her here to me. If I know anything, Rasabel will follow. I can tell her of this celestial event. If they confront the bishop when day and night converge, the curse will be broken."

"And you believe it to be so easy?"

"The signs say it is true but I have to convince Rasabel to confront the bishop."

Bylyn laughed in his face, a solid sign that she'd lost respect for the drunk man. "She intends to confront the bishop, but not with Isolde at her side. She plans to cut him through the heart and leave him bloodied and dead."

"But she must not. If she kills the bishop, the curse will never end." Intan panicked. "We cannot let that happen."

"Who would stop her?" Bylyn asked. "It isn't me." She patted her chest. "And she will certainly knock you with a fist if you try."

"There is only one person who could convince her."

"Isolde," Bylyn whispered.

He nodded. "Our beautiful Isolde." He looked to the empty corridor.

Bylyn followed his glance and stepped toward the hallway leading to the chamber where Isolde slept.

"Perhaps we can convince her of your plan?" Bylyn suggested.

He nodded, following her down the hall. "Perhaps we could." They stopped when they heard the howl of a wolf.

"Is that her?" Bylyn asked.

"She would not choose to be very far away." The bell of the drawbridge guard station rang.

"A wolf cannot ring a bell, Father." Bylyn said. "Can it?"

"Did you cover your tracks as you rode here?" he asked, scuttling toward the balcony above the bridge where he'd greeted Bylyn.

"I did not."

He handed her a dagger from his hip pouch. "Go to Isolde. Take her up the staircase to the cross-bridge. If you move quickly, you can stay ahead and escape to the forest."

"You think they are the Bishop's guards?"

He did not answer, but they both knew it was. "Go! Get her out of here now."

CHAPTER THIRTEEN

"What is left of the dream?" Isolde whispered to the flickering candle flame. The bed's cross pieces beneath her were more uncomfortable than the cold ground of the forest. The linen covering her body scratched her skin and she wanted Rasa's cloak to feel connected in some way. Her breast wound burned as the healing salve took effect, but aside from the physical discomforts, her heart hurt more than it ever had before.

For two years she'd survived without the touch of another, not realizing its absence until the girl in the forest brought her a message from the only woman she'd ever loved. This glimpse of humanity stirred emotions she'd kept buried in her solitude. She wanted to touch Rasa, talk to her, feel the intimacy that only lovers could. "I don't know how long I can bear this," she said as she closed her eyes, remembering…

"Where did you go?" Rasabel asked as she cut their path through the tall grasses of the hillside.

Isolde tittered. "I was thinking of ways to best you."

Rasa paused, sheathing her sword as she returned to Isolde's side. "Best me?" She grinned. "And how were your thoughts progressing?"

Isolde fiddled with the drawstring on her sling pouch. "It is no longer proper to say what I was thinking in public," she confessed.

"We are alone." Rasa extended her arms, making a T as she spun around. "There is only you and me here in the middle of nowhere. Tell me your secret thoughts."

Isolde's cheeks reddened. Embarrassment wasn't an emotion she often displayed, but the besting thoughts did not include the typical weapons of war. "I have been thinking of love."

"To best me with?" Rasa did not move. "You wish to best me with love while your cheeks flush the brightest crimson I've ever seen?

"Well, yes." Isolde knew her heart. She understood that hitting the center target with a rock and sling was exhilarating, and she felt those same grand quivering sensations every time Rasabel came to be in her presence.

Rasa paused, growing serious when she said, "I wish to best you with love as well." Her smile grew. "But without the crimson cheeks." She traced a finger along Isolde's hairline.

"I have come to understand these feelings... inside they were like a battlefield." Isolde looked into Rasabel's eyes, whispering, "I do not wish to fight the direction my heart is aiming. Not anymore."

"Tell me where your heart pulls you." Rasa's hand fell to Isolde's waist.

Isolde knew this was the moment and she would remember the first time she said the words, feeling them as an immortal human truth. "To you. My heart pulls me to you, and it is the only place I want to be."

Rasabel drew Isolde into her arms, holding her close. "How is it that I found you? What blessed thing have I done to bring me here to you?"

Isolde whispered against Rasa's neck, "I cannot guess. I can only wish that we will never be apart."

The wolf's howl was loud, stirring her from the dreamlike memory. The wolf was closer than Isolde expected, knowing where they were a few nights before. "You will not find me out there tonight, my love," she whispered. "Not tonight." She felt the pull of her chest wound as she tried to blow out the candle flame.

She heard the bells ringing, knowing it could mean only one thing. "They've found me." She tried to roll to her side, but forcing herself upright made her dizzy and she returned to her bed. "Is this truly how it ends?"

~~~~~~~~~~

"You were better off in the dungeon," Bylyn mumbled to herself as she ran down the corridor.
She knew Intan would take his time answering the ringing bell, like he did when she'd arrived, but whether there was time to escape would depend on the wounded woman.

The more Bylyn rushed forward, the less she could remember where the injured woman was. The ruins of the building were impossible to navigate slowly, but as she turned where she thought she'd been, she met with another dark and seemingly endless corridor. The dust-covered floors were no longer a guide as she had gone forward and back too many times.

"Isolde," she called out but silence was all she heard. She backtracked, looking for a sign of candle light. She worried the injured woman would be unconscious and, if she was, Bylyn wouldn't find her. "Isolde," she called again.

"Here. I am here." Isolde's voice was faint but still enchanting.
~~~~~~~~~~

"Call out again," Bylyn asked and made her way toward the sound, pushing every unlatched door until she found Isolde. "M'lady, I know you are not ready to travel, but we must leave," she explained hastily, relieved the woman wasn't without cover.

Isolde turned to her side, breathing through gritted teeth as she pushed herself upright. "I heard the bell. What is it? Where is Father Intan?"

"There is too much to explain right now. All I know is someone has arrived and since it cannot be the howling wolf who rang the bell, or since the moon still shines it cannot be your lady Rasa, it can only mean trouble has come for me."

Isolde gasped, not only from Bylyn's tug to pull her from the bed, but for the stranger who now understood their cursed secret. "They aren't coming for you." She fell against the wall, unsteady on her feet.

Bylyn argued, "Don't be so sure."

Isolde held back tears of pain as Bylyn's arm came around her to help her walk. The wound's herbal packing broke away, causing blood to seep again. She was weak, relying on Bylyn's strength to carry her more than support her strides.

"I'm sorry if I hurt you, but we must move quickly," Bylyn said.

"Where are we going?" With nothing on her feet, and barely a swath of fabric to cover her body, they hobbled down the long hall.

"Intan said to take the stairwell up to the top and cross the bridge to the second tower. We can escape through the tunnels below."

"I don't think I can go that far," Isolde hissed as her shoulder tensed from Bylyn's rushed advances, the drips of blood on the dust-covered hallway slowing them down and doubling the difficulty of their escape.

"We will make it. We must, or Rasabel will kill me."

Isolde chuckled at the thought. Rasabel would be in charge of bringing her here to Intan, even if her physical presence was not possible. "She does have a way about her."

"Like a bear in the woods," Bylyn joked.

Isolde gave a disapproving glance.

"A big bear, a cuddly one—one you'd feel safe with, though."

Isolde thought about Rasa, remembering the first time they had sparred with no restraint. Blade against blade, her strength against a bear of a fighter. Yes, Bylyn made a good point. "She would probably prefer a different thing of nature."

"Maybe a wolf?" Bylyn suggested.

"Yes, a wolf suits her well."

"She'd probably kill me for making such a joke, too," Bylyn added.

The strain of the wound made running difficult and Isolde paused to catch her breath.

"We can't get caught, Isolde. I've got too many powerful people trying to kill me. If we don't make it, Rasabel will be the first."

"She threatened to find you if I did not survive, didn't she?" Isolde asked.

"She told me as much when she put me on Onyx." Bylyn found the staircase. "Can you navigate these?"

"I guess we're about to find out."

Their feet fell on each stone riser, the surface cold on Isolde's feet. One after another they rose. "There's no bridge," Bylyn said as they reached the tower landing.

The ceiling above was slatted wood with a trap door and a spider-web-covered ladder leading to it.

"Can you climb a ladder?"

Isolde gripped the rung with her good arm. "Do I have a choice?"

The guards had breached the entrance bridge and their boot stomps echoed up the stairwell behind them. There was nowhere else to go.

"Climb, Isolde." Bylyn placed her body beneath the wounded woman, praying she could hold them both if Isolde slipped. Her heart was racing, blood pumping, and her only defense was her bare hands and an imaginative ability to lie. It was impossible to believe they would win this fight if there wasn't a bridge connected to this tower.

With her head as the only means to push the trap door, Isolde thrust the panel over. The glow of the moon was their only light, but there was nothing to see.

"There is no bridge, Bylyn." There was panic in the delivery of this news. The tower platform was bare. "We are defenseless."

"In the tower!" a guard yelled, and Bylyn heard their boots clomping to find them.

"They are coming." Bylyn slammed the trap door hard, pushing the toggle into place. "It will not hold," she said.

Isolde held their bodies together, adding their weight for good measure. From their position overhead, she could see Intan unconscious, Rasa's bow and arrow quiver beside him on the ground. "Get closer," she said and felt the piercing pain of her wound.

A sword stabbed through the slatted trap door. Bylyn jumped to avoid the blade, knocking Isolde backward over the tower ledge.

Until this moment in her short life, Bylyn didn't believe she had an honorable purpose. She moved in the world from place to place, never really investing in another human being. Her heart nearly stopped as she watched Isolde disappear over the waist-high wall. She stretched her body, diving across to follow, gripping Isolde by the forearm of her flailing wounded side.

Their eyes met and words to undo their predicament could not be said as they realized neither had the strength to undo this mistake.

Can a tragedy become more tragic? Bylyn thought. She felt the sweat dripping from her face, dropping like a first raindrop to land thirty feet below.

"Don't let me fall," Isolde begged, doing her best not to kick or flail as the bright red stain of blood gobbled the pale color of her makeshift frock.

Bylyn struggled to keep her footing as the tower brick gouged her ribs and hips.

Isolde slipped little by little, down Bylyn's sweaty forearm, begging with her eyes not to fall.

It was a look that Bylyn would never forget, an absolute understanding that her life belonged to the other but it would not end happily. Their positions should have been reversed—Isolde could have tossed the girl back up —but fate was cruel to them both.

"Give me your other hand," Bylyn pleaded.

Isolde tried to grip Bylyn but the sway made her slide away. "I'm slipping."

Bylyn squeezed, unable to stop the pull of the earth, unable to look away as the moment happened behind the eyes, deep in the soul, where Isolde's desperate fear took on life.

Forearm… "M'lady," Bylyn begged.

Wrist… "I cannot hold you."

Hand… Isolde's eyes grew wide. "Bylyn!"

Knuckles… Desperate for a miracle, Bylyn tried to use her second hand.

Fingertips… "Tell her I love her."

Bylyn was certain her heart stopped as Isolde fell from her fingers. The scream was unlike anything she had ever heard and she never wished to experience it again.

Isolde's body did not dash against the rocks below. Bylyn could not believe her eyes as the woman's arms and body disappeared into the screeching, feathered bird. The blood-stained fabric twisted and swirled through the air like a ribbon. The sight would have been inspirational if not for the thundering of her heart. The guards were about to breach the tower door, but at least Isolde, in her animal form, was safe. She would die knowing her promise to Rasa had been kept, hoping this honorable deed would take her to a fruitful afterlife.

She climbed over the tower ledge to an ornamental forest sprite statue. *Ironic*, she thought as she wedged herself tightly. If she was lucky it would hold her weight, but there was nowhere to shelter from the tip of a long sword.

The soldiers breached the door. "Where are they? I saw there were two."

The second soldier leaned over the edge. "One is here." He stabbed his sword down at her.

"Where is the other?" he asked, his blade tip inches away from striking Bylyn.

"She's gone." Bylyn kicked her heels into the statue, smashing herself against the tower wall to avoid the blade.

"Liar, where is she?" He circled the tower edge, searching for the second person, leaning over to see a body.

"I swear to all the goddesses and gods, she flew away." Bylyn had never been so happy to be this compact size, as it was this tininess keeping her from the sword's blows.

He raised his blade, hoping the high strike would cut her down. "Liars must go. I don't care what the bishop ordered."

Bylyn heard the whir of an arrow's fletching spiraling through the air. She could not see its target until the guard's body passed on the way to the rocks below.

Two more arrows flew and Bylyn looked down, expecting Intan, but instead seeing the physically imposing Rasabel, naked, bowstring drawn tight to her cheek. Fearlessly stripped bare of protections, the warrior loosed the arrow, dropped the bow to the ground and spun toward a new attacker.

Bylyn wanted to call out a warning, but Rasa didn't miss a maneuver as she sidestepped the guard's sword strike, kicked hard with her bare foot, knocking the blade to the ground. Rasa rolled, spinning to her feet. With sword in hand, she struck the man once across the arm, severing it at the shoulder. Rasa's right-side pivot followed with a striking blow to the throat, slicing the man's head cleanly from his neck.

The sound that followed was the heaving scream of Rasabel's victory, terrifying and thrilling at the same time.

Clenching to the tower ornamentation seemed courageous to Bylyn until she witnessed the sight below: a warrior stripped of every protection, wearing the blood of her enemies, running toward the tower.

Moments later, a bristly rope dropped over the ledge.

"You are safe, now," Rasa yelled. "Take hold."

Bylyn could not speak, so shaken from the experience it took two tries before she could lean far enough to reach the rope. It did not escape her that only minutes ago she'd nearly leaped over to save Isolde. Bylyn did her best to wrap the rope around her body.

"Are you secure?" Rasa asked.

Bylyn tugged the knot. "As much as I can be."

Without another word, the slack pulled tight and the little thief was raised to safety.

Rasa held a hand to help Bylyn stand, but the girl did not move. "Thank you," she gasped.

"We should check on Intan," was all Rasa said as she raced down the rails of the ladder. The woman didn't pause to ask questions or to hear the thank you that Bylyn whispered again.

Bylyn lay on her back, her hand resting on her chest as her heartbeat pounded hard against it. "What has happened here? I do not understand." She huffed.

As if in response, the hawk squawked as it circled overhead. There was inexplicable magic in Rasabel and Isolde's world, and Bylyn was forever a part of it. "She is a hawk who loves a wolf." Bylyn thought saying it aloud would make it feel true, but it only made her complicated world more unreal.

"What have I done?" The rope around her breasts felt like a stranglehold as she struggled to untangle it from her body. "Impossible."

CHAPTER FOURTEEN

There were two things Bylyn never imagined she'd see in her life. One was a naked woman covered in blood, and the other was a man shoving a naked woman away.

She wanted to escape this nightmare but it ran like a raging river into her days. It was becoming a common thing to see her companions unclothed, but until now she had shied away from truly looking at Rasabel's body. Rasabel wore many old scars across her chest and back, but Bylyn was most curious about the puckered purple mark on the warrior's thigh, the same spot where the arrow had landed.

Bylyn was staring now, but was unable to look away, red-faced by the realization it could be misread as lecherous gawking.

"You stubborn fool," Rasa scolded. "Let me help you." Standing naked, wearing the blood of her enemies, it was no surprise the man did not want her to touch him.

"I can make it on my own." Intan pushed her away. "I may be old and tired, but I'm not a fragile piece of glass."

Rasabel stepped aside, staying close enough to catch his stumble.

Bylyn watched, curious and uneasy about the behavior of these two, and happy to know her stare went unnoticed. Before the betrayal of this curse, there had been something between Intan and Rasabel, a friendship perhaps, but there wasn't much of that left now.

Eventually noticing the girl, Rasa stopped. Bylyn expected an inquiry about her well-being but instead the naked woman asked, "How is Onyx?"

"She's there, in the stable. You can see for yourself. I have delivered everything as you asked," Bylyn answered, thinking it odd that the warrior would be worried about the horse instead of her.

"And my saddle bags?"

"I am fine, in case you're wondering." Bylyn made her way to the pile hidden beneath the tattered blanket. "Here, I have not stolen any of your things." Her emotions tumbled from curiosity to anger at the idea she would steal from Rasa in her time of need.

"It's not that, little thief." Rasa chuckled. "As immodest as you might think I am." She waved over her bloody naked torso. "I require washing and fresh clothes before we discuss the happenings of the last hour."

"Oh." Bylyn's lips made a humbled loose circle. "Yes, why didn't I think of that?"

Intan mopped at the blood on his brow. "Distracted, I suppose," he teased as he limped toward the dining hall. His goal was simple: slather his wound with what was left of the healing salve he'd mixed for Isolde.

"Where do you wash, old man?" Rasa's question had an angry bite, filled with resentment born from betrayal. She disliked needing anything from her former confessor.

"The moat pool is spring fed." He pointed toward the stairwell to the lower corridors. "Follow the sound of water."

Rasabel draped the saddlebag over her shoulder and followed Intan's instructions.

"She is angry," Intan said as he fell onto the bench.

Bylyn took the bowl of salve from his hand. "We saved Isolde. She should be happy."

"It isn't Isolde," he said. "It's being here. It's that she had to ask for help from me."

"I understand," Bylyn said. "After the last few hours, and the story you shared, I don't like you very much either."

~~~~~~~~~~

Rasa dropped her saddlebag on the edge of the walk-in bathing reservoir. The towels hanging on the line were stiff but surprisingly clean compared to the rest of the crumbling surroundings. The blood on her hands stood in sharp contrast to the gray of the towel linen. "What a morning." She tugged a washing rag from the line.

The sound of a bird's wings cut the air, gaining her attention. The animal drifted in through the open wall and flapped twice to hover before dropping down, its talons
~~~~~~~~~~

digging into the leather of the saddlebag. Rasa had never been so happy to see her hawk fly.

"Hello, love." Rasa smiled. "It seems you and our little thief had quite a sunrise." As she spoke to the bird, the animal's head dipped side to side as if she would respond.

Rasa stepped into the water. "Ooh, this is cold." She rubbed her arms. There was no easing in as she slipped off the bottom step. After the shock subsided, the icy temperature soothed her battle-sore body. She plunged the swath of fabric into the pool and began washing the blood from her skin.

"The Bishop's people sure do bleed an awful lot," she grumbled before diving beneath the surface to rinse herself clean. After two years in the wilderness, surviving on skill and intuition, she was an expert at washing battle from her body. It was her soul that grew tired, and she wished the pain of life without her lover was something she could wash away.

She swam through the water, popping up inches from where the animal sat waiting for her to surface. "Do not fear, I'll be here for you." She reached to stroke the bird's face. "Eternally, my love will not fail."

There was no mutual exchange of the sentiment, but Rasa trusted that somewhere inside the bird, Isolde knew. She wondered how her lost love made it through the long nights alone. She rested her chin on her forearm, stroking the bird's feathered breast. "There is no sign of your injury."

The bird leaned into the touch.

"It will be two years." Rasa wiped the tear from her cheek and it disappeared in the water bath. "I miss you," she whispered, remembering their goodbyes…

*"Will you miss me when I leave?"
Rasa asked and Isolde looked away. "Is?"
She could not read her lover's expression.*

*"You see where we are?" Isolde's
response was sharp. It was a stupid
question for Rasa to ask after the passion
they'd shared. Isolde felt many things about
her lover, but the thought of adding missing
her to the list cut deep.*

*"Isolde." Rasa turned to rest on her
forearm. They were half-dressed, garments
askew from the desperate need to touch.*

*"You ask me if I'll miss you when my
body still heaves from our love making,"
Isolde whispered. "I know what will happen
if your friend cannot marry us. I will become
someone I do not wish to know."*

*"I will not let them—let him—have
you." It was clear the warrior meant to back
those words with every fighting skill she
possessed.*

"You will fight them all for me?"

*"For us," Rasa insisted as she pulled
the woman on top of her.*

*"Then, yes," Isolde answered to a
confused Rasabel.*

"Yes?"

*Isolde smiled as her mouth paused
above her lover's. "Yes, I would miss you. I
miss you when you leave my sight. I miss*

you when I close my eyes to sleep but I never want to miss you for a single day if I get to choose."

"If I get to choose." Rasa whispered the memory. The bird squawked, breaking Rasa from her melancholy. There was no time to get lost in what was. She jumped from the water to the ledge of the bathing pool, her body dripping and her hair tangled to the ends.

The day the curse was cast, Rasa swore two things: to avenge the bishop's evil, and to remain true to her appearance so Isolde would know her wherever they went after this life. She hadn't cut her hair. The scars of a soldier's life were there, mapped and memorized in intimate moments, altered only by those acquired while surviving this curse. Isolde would know her, she believed. Nothing would be different if they ever met again.

She tugged a towel from the line. "Let's go see what our thief and betrayer have to say." She rubbed the scratchy fabric over her body before putting on the last of her fresh clothes. "Perhaps our little thief deserves something to wear, too."

~~~~~~~~~~

"Will you stop pulling away?" Bylyn tipped the man's head toward the fluttering torch flame. The daylight coming from the windows in the dining hall wasn't enough for her to check his wound for debris.

"You're rubbing too hard," he grumbled. "Can't you have a gentle touch, you clomping cow?"
~~~~~~~~~~

Bylyn scoffed. "As if I'm a cow. I hardly eat every three days and truth be told I can sneak in and out of almost anywhere unlike a cow that clomps."

"Is that how you landed in the dungeons of Acadia?"

They turned toward the sound of Rasabel's question. The woman's presence was impressive, if not breathtaking; she stood with a hawk digging talons deep into the heavy leather of the saddle bag on her shoulder, looking fresh, as if they hadn't fought off a half dozen of the Bishop's guards an hour before.

"I'll have you know"—Bylyn wagged her salve-covered finger between the two—"I was caught because a man saw me take a loaf of bread."

"And this is your great skill?" Intan grumbled as he leaned away from her less-than-gentle touch. "It certainly isn't dressing a wound."

Rasa stepped closer. "Let me have a look." The hawk leapt to the top rung of the high-backed chair. The crossbar dipped, the lopsided angle causing the bird to flap her wings to right her balance.

"There's nothing to see." Intan shoved their hands away.

"I put the herbs on." Bylyn defended how she cleaned and dressed his wound. "It's not as though we can do anything more."

"It looks good, but there will be a scar."

Intan groaned as he stood. "What's one more?" He tipped the cup on the table, knocking the remnants from last night's drink on the floor. Bylyn thought he would fill it with water but the old man poured a hefty cup of wine.

"You're still an old fool." Rasa watched him guzzle half the cup of liquid. "Still owned by the drink." She grabbed it from his hand. "I have something to say before I lose you to that." She set the cup on the table.

"What?" He could not meet her eyes. "Judge me if you must."

Rasabel pulled on her gloves, ready to leave this cursed place. "I cannot—"

"You don't think I judge myself?" he interrupted.

The hawk flapped her wings in response, blowing the dust from the table on all of them. Rasabel paused. It had been two years since she'd stood before this man to make a vow of forever love with Isolde at her side. His betrayal was their demise; instead of loving her new wife into the day and night, they fell under the power of this terrible curse.

"I don't care what you do, old man." She raised her hand out to the bird and she leapt onto it. "But you saved her last night, and for that I am eternally grateful."

Intan paused with the cup to his lips. Fate led to the discovery, a way to bring the lovers back together to live a human life again. In his heart he knew it was not a coincidence that they were here in his home. The bishop's lust had torn them apart but the priest knew how to end the curse.

He had to tell Rasabel, so he followed her outside. "Her wound is a second chance." He raised the cup with a trembling hand and took a sip.

Rasa stopped, pivoting around to confront the madness violating her ears. "A second chance at what?" She studied the grounds, looking for signs of wounded guards, as she spun her back to the wall. "What have you done, Intan?"

"Four nights ago, I had a dream."

Rasa walked away, releasing the bird to fly. "We've been on the receiving end of your nightmare. I'll not hear of your dreams."

Intan dropped his cup, reaching for Rasabel's arm. "You must listen. I have seen it." He tried to turn her around, but she was too strong. "I know how to break the curse."

Rasa pulled away. "The curse!" she yelled, leaning close to his face. "You helped the monster put that curse on us. On her!" She directed them skyward to watch the hawk circling. "How?" Her voice broke from heartache. "How could you put a curse on her?"

Intan could not look into the sky, knowing what he would see and how it would destroy what little he had left to live for. "I was weak." His stare begged for absolution as he confessed, "I was a fool."

"And you damned us to this torturous half-life." Her fist clenched, but she did not strike. "You'll find no forgiveness in me." She turned.

"And for Isolde?" He dared to say her name.

Rasabel stepped hard and fast and wrapped her hands around his neck. "Do not say her name. Do not speak to me again of this tale you tell from a drunken man's dream." She pushed him away, eager to escape this trap of fate.

"What if that dream brings her back to you?"

"You've lost yourself to that wine, old man." Rasa walked away. "And you're a fool." She found her hawk resting on the horn of Onyx's saddle. She tossed the bag from her shoulder and began dressing the horse.

Intan startled her when he said, "I know how to break the curse."

Rasa pulled her sword from the sheath. "This is how you break a curse."

"No!" he yelled.

"The bishop will feel my blade and I will look him in the eyes as I push it through his cold, dead heart." She slid the sword forward, mimicking the stabbing move.

"If you kill the bishop, the curse remains unchanged." Intan's eyes were wide as two full moons. "Think of your wife."

Rasa stilled. It had been two long years without hearing that word, without identifying as the word, without feeling the intimacy of two becoming one. This man knew too much; he had too much power to break her already splintered heart.

She pushed him with a force of rage from too many lost moments. "My wife!" Spit flew from her mouth as she yelled, "My wife sits on her perch. She squawks and flies and I have not looked upon her face in two years." She sheathed her sword. "My wife lives a life without me and I without her." Her hands trembled as she buckled her weapon into the harness of the saddle bag.

The bird circled overhead, a constant reminder of what was lost.

"I trained for ten years to become battle-ready for anything." Rasa studied the hawk's flight. "But not for…" She cleared her throat, feeling too vulnerable. "Don't try to define what my duties are to Isolde. I live my days for her." The leather squealed as Rasabel kicked onto her saddle. "Do not speak to me of this again, Intan. Stay here with your drink and rot."

"Rasabel," Bylyn called, and the warrior stopped. "Do I travel with you?"

Tears streamed from Rasa's eyes and she did not turn around. "Stay or go, little thief. You have earned your freedom." She tapped her heels against Onyx's side. "My life is worse than the prison you escaped." She could offer the girl nothing but sorrow now that the truth was out. They were miles from Acadia and with no guards left to share details of the lost fight, the thief would be safe here with Intan.

Bylyn was shocked, watching Rasa ride away as if her sacrifice to save Isolde was the end.

"Go, go with her." Intan pushed the girl. "I will follow when I can and speak with Isolde," he whispered.

"Rasabel," Bylyn called, doing her best to downplay Intan's sudden proposition. "I will go with you. There's nothing for me here."

"Catch up, little thief," Rasa yelled.

Bylyn winked at the priest to let him know she liked this new plan. "Follow us soon," she whispered as she stumbled over her flopping boots in a hurry to catch up with the lone rider.

CHAPTER FIFTEEN

Bylyn stumbled as she turned to look back for the castle ruins. Although her feet had recovered from stepping on pebbles and briars during the prison escape, her floppy boots were making it difficult to keep up with the angry warrior. She could no longer see the ruins Intan called home. The sun was past its high point and she knew if they continued at this pace, they were a few days' journey from Acadia. If the priest were to intersect with them, she needed to impede their progress.

"I'd appreciate it if we could go slower," Bylyn said as she jogged alongside Rasabel. "I've run every day since I was a little girl." She was babbling, she knew, but she was also trying to get the stubborn woman to talk to her, and distract her from this single-sighted mission. She looked ahead at the thicket and the tree line coming into view. Navigating a forest would help to slow things down.

In the last twelve hours, Bylyn had witnessed unbelievable happenings and she needed to talk, not only about the naked woman, or the maimed hawk, or the drunken priest, but how all of the experiences rested so easily in her imaginative thoughts. But she could not do that as she ran alongside the focused warrior.

So she babbled. "I was mostly running away," she continued, holding up a finger to add, "I wasn't always running from trouble though. I delivered goods in the village."

Rasa chuckled. As annoying as Bylyn was, talking nonstop for the last few hours, she was also entertaining. "What kind of goods does a thief deliver?" she asked.

Surprised by the woman's question, Bylyn stumbled over the answer. "Well..." She had to think because she didn't truly help anyone but herself. "I got bread from the baker and I would deliver it to the innkeeper." She did not share that the bread was stolen and that she took a coin from the innkeeper for it. "Fruit from the orchard that I would take to the innkeeper. Things like that."

"And did this innkeeper understand the source of your goods?" Rasa asked.

Bylyn shrugged. "We never discussed such things."

"Whoa," Rasa said, pulling on the reins before kicking a foot over the horn and sliding off her saddle.

Bylyn stumbled back as Rasa pulled her blade. She did not advance at the statue-still Bylyn; instead the sword tip hit the ground, stabbing into a thick patch of brush.

"That's quite a skill." Bylyn gulped, taking a large step backward. Her fear was palpable as she was reminded that the former Captain of the Guard *was* the former Captain of the Guard.

Rasa raised her blade, displaying a furry animal skewered to the tip. "Dinner," was all she said, completely unaware of how frightening her hunting tactic was. With the smoothest motion, she sliced a hind leg from the animal and raised it up in the air. The hawk swooped down, taking the piece from Rasa's outstretched hand. "She needs to eat."

Bylyn's heart raced, but she was curious. "Doesn't she hunt on her own?" she asked.

"You ask a lot of questions, little thief." Rasa wiped her blade with the sash tucked in her belt before returning it to the sheath.

"Aye, I guess I do, and you hardly ever answer any of them."

Rasa shrugged. "I suppose you're right. I've been alone for a long time, little thief. Silence is a hazard of solitude, I suppose."

"I wish you would stop calling me that," Bylyn said.

Rasa snickered. "So what do they call you if not a thief?"

"My name is Bylyn. They call me that, or..." She crossed her arms defiantly.

"Or?"

Bylyn hesitated to answer because if kind words were spoken, they were rarely about her.

Rasa kicked at the patch of dirt on the ground as she made space to clean the rabbit. "Come on, now, it can't be that bad."

"What if it is?" Bylyn realized Rasa was going to cook what was left of the animal, and began collecting sticks from the tree line.

"I have been called many things in my life, little thief. Yours could not be as bad." Rasa skinned the animal and laid it in the grass.

"What have *you* been called?" Bylyn asked, hopeful the terms were equally embarrassing.

Rasabel kicked through the brush along the tree line, finding pieces of fallen limb to make a fire. "Beast." She paused to think. "Brute." She chuckled. "That one was true, still is." She snapped the limbs over her knee, affirming her strength was not imaginary.

"Brute was not my first thought when I saw you," Bylyn said.

Rasa looked up from fire making. "Tell me what it was?" she asked.

"Warrior." Bylyn smiled. "You attacked that crowd of guards as if they were nothing of consequence."

Rasa struck two flint stones together, making a spark to light her tinder. "It turned out they mostly were." She grinned. "If I'd trained them, it would have been more of a fight."

"So my name stands." Bylyn dropped her sticks. "You are a warrior."

Rasabel skewered the dressed animal while waiting for the fire to blaze. "I have had no choice but to be many things in the last two years," she said.

"I suppose you have." The silence that followed was uncomfortable for Bylyn, and she waited for the warrior to share more.

Rasa blew across the tinder. "Now that you know some of my unusual titles, tell me some of yours."

"Imp." Bylyn squatted beside the fire waiting for the woman's reaction.

Rasa was expecting more. "That's it?" She worked the base of the skewer into the ground, propping it against a split timber for roasting.

"It's a horrible thing to be called." She snaked a summoning finger. "Come here, little imp." She made a dismissive hand gesture. "Deliver the bread, little imp. Go away, little imp."

Rasa asked, "Is it horrible to be called an imp because you are little or because you manage to get into mischief?"

Bylyn stepped to the horse, unbuckling the sword and saddle bags and passing them to Rasa. It was obvious they would camp on the edge of the forest for the night, so she made the horse more comfortable. "It is horrible because I am no devil or goblin." She stood, stiffly asserting her position. "Yes, I make mischief but only to survive. If I had a roof and a place to call home I might not need to be a thief."

"Sprite," Rasa said with no explanation.

Bylyn ducked to the ground, looking for such a creature to appear. "Where?"

Rasa rotated the cooking meat. "You." She tipped the skewer at Bylyn. "Little sprite, and I mean that with the utmost respect."

Bylyn wrinkled her nose, annoyed by the idea. "That name reduces me to a thing from children's folklore."

"Yes." Rasa looked up, making certain Bylyn was paying attention as she said, "Being reduced to a creature of myth and lore is something I understand."

Bylyn could not argue against the statement; for the warrior, it was true. Rasa was half human and half beast, but always something to fear. The silence that followed spoke of a common understanding that the pair existed in an unchosen and cursed story.

Bylyn prepared for a night with Isolde, while Rasabel cooked a meal she would not get to enjoy. The sun was close to setting as Bylyn tore a leg from the roasted animal. She was hungry, but also curious to witness the rotation of the women she found her life tethered to. She hoped Intan was somewhere on the horizon, close behind them, waiting for the moon to become their evening light.

"It is time for me to go, Little Sprite," Rasa said as she folded the cloak, leaving it atop the saddle. She had done this exchange from human to animal more times than she wanted to count and still she was unsettled.

"I'll keep watch over her," Bylyn vowed.

Rasa chuckled as she removed her riding pants. With a single motion, she swept the linen shirt over her head, like hundreds of times before. There was no embarrassment about her nudity. "Don't underestimate Isolde. She's very good in a fight and she might keep an eye on you first."

Bylyn tried not to be obvious as she admired her battle-scarred physique. Rasa was the definition of a warrior, and a linen shirt did very little to change that.

Rasa folded the clothes inside the saddle bag, removing some for Isolde to wear.

"See you in the morning," Bylyn said as Rasa disappeared into the forest.

A voice echoed through the trees. "Until tomorrow, Little Sprite."

~~~~~~~~~~

Bylyn stumbled to her feet as she heard the snapping twigs. "Intan?" she whispered but the voice that answered was not the grumble of a stumbling man.

"Not this time," Isolde smirked. "Just a woman who caught the scent of dinner." She stepped from the shadows, her lean pale skin the perfect opposite of the woman who loved her.

There was a scar on Isolde's chest where the arrow had pierced it, and Bylyn could not stop her stare. *What an impossible thing to see*, she thought. "Your wife prepared this dinner before she disappeared into the trees."

Isolde stopped, her hands clutching the clothes on the saddle. For two years she had yearned to hear those words said aloud. "My wife," she whispered. Bylyn's phrase was delivered innocently, yet was careless in the way it caught Isolde off guard.

"Yes," Bylyn explained, adding her spin to the conversation. "I vowed to take care of you when she left."

"Vowed." Isolde chuckled. It was ridiculous to think after two years she could not care for herself but she let Bylyn have her moment. "You made a vow with Rasa... to take care of me... really?" She slipped the shirt over her head. "*You*"—she pointed between them—"will take care of *me*?"
~~~~~~~~~~

"I declare it is true." Bylyn held a hand over her heart. "She made me swear to be your charge."

"To be my charge?" Isolde's eyebrow peaked. "How have I survived all this time without my mighty and great protector?"

"Rasa wondered the same, which is why I swore the oath."

"To take care and be my charge?"

Bylyn smiled. "Exactly."

"Well, to take care of me means we should eat this dinner and not let it go to waste."

"My thoughts, too." Bylyn held the skewer to Isolde.

They sat in silence as, little by little, the roasted rabbit disappeared. The fire was warm against the cooling night and a wolf's howl broke the silence.

"You're very quiet," Bylyn said, craving conversation.

Isolde tossed the bone into the fire. It had been so long since she'd spoken to someone who knew her connection to the animal howling nearby. "I am always alone," she said. "If I talk to myself in the dark, the spirits might come for me, so I sit and I think."

"What do you think about?" Bylyn asked.

Isolde didn't answer, certain that her true thoughts would frighten the girl away.

"M'lady," Bylyn said.

Isolde turned to her, tears sliding down her cheeks. She did not bother to swipe them away. "This is not the life I dreamed of," she said. "I did not wish to be a lover or wife. I wished to be a warrior."

This confession was not what Bylyn expected to hear and the girl didn't know what to say. "But you met Captain Rasabel."

Isolde released an unsteady breath, "I met Captain Rasabel," she whispered, "and I was never the same again." Tears dripped from her chin, disappearing in the dirt by her tucked legs. "She was larger than any life I ever dreamed."

"Yes." Bylyn chuckled. "I have met her, she is exactly that and maybe a little more."

Isolde's tears trailed along a serious frown. "I disliked her at first; the command she had over herself was frustrating, and I fought my heart's pull to her."

"She says you are a strong fighter," Bylyn interrupted.

"Not strong enough to resist her love." Isolde pulled her knees to her chest.

"No one could," Bylyn confessed and it was the first smile she saw Isolde make.

"You have fallen under her love spell, too," Isolde teased.

It was not Rasa that Bylyn admired, but the way Rasa loved Isolde. Bylyn had never met anyone who would give everything for intimacy they could not have in the flesh. Isolde was a walking dream and Bylyn, like Rasabel, would do anything to keep her safe. "I have great admiration for her, yes."

Isolde stared at the flickering flames, desperate to ask a question and afraid of the answer. "How is she?"

Bylyn stammered, "Your Rasabel?"

Isolde nodded, unable to speak her wife's name.

"She is well." With the heat from the fire fading, Bylyn drew the sword from the sheath to chop the collected limbs into smaller pieces. She huffed after a few swings, the blade growing too heavy for the task.

"You said she was hit with an arrow." Isolde grabbed the sword on Bylyn's backswing, disarming her easily. "And her wound?" She made quick work of the chopping task with six solid swings. "How is the wound?"

"She's much like you are tonight. Her animal form has the same healing powers as yours."

Isolde sheathed the sword. "Yes, it is a curious thing." She rubbed her hand across her breast, knowing that since the curse began there were many scars beneath the shirt she wore.

"You are very lucky," Bylyn said as she tossed a scrap of tree limb on the fire, making sparks dance high.

"Am I?"

"I mean, to have a wife like you do," Bylyn said, her envy of the relationship obvious in her tone.

"She—," Isolde hesitated, realizing this person beside her had spent more time with her wife in the last two days than she'd spent in the two years since their marriage ceremony.

"She is worried about you," Bylyn shared.

Isolde sat beside Bylyn. "She has said so?"

"She has." Bylyn covered her heart. "I swear."

"Yes, you swear… and is this worry the reason she is taking us to Acadia?"

Bylyn hesitated.

"You must tell me."

The sorrow in Isolde's voice was painful to Bylyn's ears but she did not answer. How could she explain the warrior's thirst to take a holy leader's life, even if the man had damned theirs?

The howl of a wolf broke the silence, followed by a yelp and whimpering from pain.

"What was that?" Bylyn asked.

"A wolf's cry." Isolde slipped her sword over her shoulder and patted her belt to check for her sling as she raced into the forest. "It's in pain." She only had Rasa's wolf form in mind and did not look behind her for the girl. She swiped a rock from the ground before hitting her full stride toward the animal in distress.

Bylyn scrambled to unfasten the bow, and fumbled through every arrow trying to get one from the quiver as she chased after Isolde. She had no skill with the weapon but maybe the threat of holding it would intimidate enough.

Isolde snuck up on the site, unsure what she was seeing. A wolf stood upright, acting like a human but not like Rasa. This creature had hands. Hands holding a dagger that was slicing the belly of a brown and white colored wolf.

She crept closer, silently, as she moved for a better view. She saw a chin protruding from the wolf-head mask he wore. The man was no mystical being. He was another blood-thirsty hunting monster.

Isolde released her breath, relieved this was not Rasa but also intent on preventing him from finding her love. Bylyn's approach was noisy, her boots clomping, snapping twigs and litter on the forest floor.

The hunter looked up to see Isolde in the shadows. "What is this?"

Isolde twisted the sling loop around her finger. "This is no one," she said as she tucked the rock into the leather pocket.

The hunter dropped the animal. "No one looks like she is alone." He licked his lips, advancing toward Isolde.

"I'm alone, too." He swirled his dagger like a pointing stick. "Perhaps we can be alone, together," he sniggered.

"Isolde," Bylyn yelled as she stumbled into the fight, the bowstring drawn as tight against her cheek as she could hold it. She had no skill with the weapon, had never shot one or even held one in a fight, but she was determined to look menacing.

"Isolde," the man repeated. "Delicious name, Isolde. I have heard that name before."

"Bylyn, go back," Isolde yelled, never taking her eyes off the hunter as her rotating sling cut through the air.

"M'lady," Bylyn argued, "I have sworn a vow." She felt the tension of the bowstring's draw fatiguing her muscles.

The hunter laughed. "Another one of you. My night just got two times better."

Isolde did not advance, instead waiting for the man to make a move. The tangle of saplings parted behind the hunter, as the black wolf approached, white teeth bared and ready to devour.

"And there you are," the hunter snarled, nearly giddy with excitement to find what he'd been hunting for in the darkness. "The Bishop said where you find Isolde of Mondurey, you will find the black wolf, and it has been most satisfactory to hunt for the two of you by moonlight."

"There are three of us now." Bylyn loosed the arrow but it did not fly. Instead, the fletching caught the back of her hand, slicing her thumb. The string slapped her unprotected forearm, vibrating the bow from her grip.

The hunter sidestepped the arrow, where it lay in the grass, and hit the girl with the bloody club of his hand.

Bylyn crumbled to the ground.

"Now it's your turn." He drew a sword, expecting Isolde to quiver in fear but she stood confidently, waiting to release the stone in the whirring sling.

The wolf growled, circling until it was close to Isolde's hip. The hunter underestimated the animal's size and stepped back. Isolde released the stone, striking the hunter's face and knocking him backward over Bylyn's unconscious body. The fight was almost unfair—Isolde struck hard and then the wolf, sensing weakness, moved in to take control. It lunged at the man, knocking the sword away, attacking easily to tear at the hunter's throat. Blood sprayed as the man's eyes went wide. The shocked expression changed seconds later as fear froze on his face.

Isolde drew her sword, pointing it at the hunter's chest. "You were hardly a fight," she said as she watched life drain from his eyes.

The wolf sniffed at the corpse before wandering over to investigate the scent of the recently-slaughtered animal. Her howl echoed through the trees, silhouetted by the light of the moon, reminding Isolde that the creature was more inhuman than human.

Isolde cried, not for the death of the foul man but for the life she was forced to live without Rasabel. She sheathed her sword and collected her sling from the ground.

"Bylyn." Isolde tapped the girl's cheek but she did not wake. She leveraged the girl onto her shoulder and carried her back to camp. She did not worry about the wolf or the hunter's bodies, trusting the creatures of the night to take care of their remains.

"Cold water would do for that lump," Isolde said as she searched the saddlebag for a piece of cloth. "Will this nightmare ever end?" She stared at her camp and the girl on the ground. She did not want her life to include this child, she was no substitute for a lover and partner. "What will I do?"

CHAPTER SIXTEEN

Rasa woke by the edge of the forest. Her mouth was dry and she felt more disconnected from herself than ever in the last two years. Perhaps it was the injury to Isolde the day before or it was her mind fighting for any memory of the unstoppable transformations. Either way, waking in unknown places was taking a toll, and concerns for Bylyn were an added complication.

Rasa was covered in blood, again—this time from whatever she'd done in animal form. She despised that she could not retrieve those memories in the light of day. With no water for washing, she rubbed the dew-covered leaves over her arms.

She followed the scent of fire, searching for her horse and hoping her new travel companion was with it. Her hawk was nowhere in sight, but that was common and dependent upon where and when their lives intersected at dawn. She hadn't felt vulnerable about her nakedness for months, but noticed Bylyn's reaction when she disrobed the night before. She would need to pay attention when arriving at camp.

Bylyn was asleep when Rasa entered camp. She sidestepped the girl, making her way to the clothes she'd left behind the day before. Her fingers traveled across the corded stitching along the edge of her cloak. It was folded differently from the way she'd left it, and her heart hurt knowing it had touched her lover's body. She pressed it to her face, searching for a hint of Isolde in the no-longer-plush fabric. "This is almost the rag you claimed it to be," she whispered, remembering that intimate moment…

"You never tire of wearing the same old rag?" Isolde teased as she mounted her horse. Rasa was beside her, grinning as she did when they were together and alone.

"Old rag?" Rasa adjusted in her saddle, waving the heavy fabric to billow around her. "This cloak is more than an old rag."

"Is that so?" Isolde teased as she nudged the horse forward.

"It is," Rasa replied. "This rag, as you call it, has brought comfort in the cold."

Isolde smirked at what was an obvious use for a cloak. "Most cloaks do that."

"Yes, but this one gives me shelter from the wind"—Rasa held the corners up over her head—"and from the rain."

"I'm sure your horse appreciates such covering," Isolde added playfully.

Rasabel nodded. "Yes, she does. But it has another use, my favorite use that makes me keep this old rag."

"And what might that be?" Isolde asked.

"This old rag is plush on the inside, making it the softest place to lay with a lover."

Isolde blushed. "Oh."

"Yes." Rasa grinned.

Surprised and intrigued by this intimate disclosure, Isolde asked. "Have you laid with many lovers on that rag?"

Rasabel laughed. "An honorable lover would never share such things."

"So that is a yes." Isolde twisted in her saddle to watch Rasabel squirm.

"That is a non answer, Isolde of Mondurey. Surely you would not want me to share such information if the lover was you."

"If the lover was me, I would already know the answer."

"Yes, I suppose you would," Rasabel conceded.

Isolde tugged the reins of Rasa's horse, stopping them on the riding path.

She reached for the cloak, a wicked grin flushing her cheek as she rubbed the fabric between her hands. She leaned in to whisper and Rasabel swallowed hard at the sudden closeness. "I have to agree, it is indeed plush." Her eyebrow peaked. "And yet"—her lips were a breath away—"it is still a bit of a rag." She brushed her lips against the captain's cheek.

Before Rasa could react to the intimacy, Isolde rode away, stealing the moment, winning the argument and capturing Rasabel's heart.

"A rag indeed," Rasa said as she pulled the shirt over her head, wishing more than anything to be in that moment again.

"Rasabel?" Bylyn called out in a groggy voice.

"Give me a minute, Little Sprite, and we will pack up camp." The cherished memory broken, Rasa fumbled her shirt over her head and dressed for another day of travel.

"Might I rest a little longer?" Bylyn asked, feeling the pain in her forearm and the rise of swelling on her head wound.

Rasa turned to look at the girl, ready to protest the request until she noticed the lump on her head, the slash on her hand and the dark bruise on her forearm. She looked for the hawk and was relieved when she found her perched on the tree beside the girl. The bird had not greeted her this morning, and now she understood the animal was watching their little sprite. "What happened to you?"

Bylyn touched the bump on her head. "This is nothing." She stumbled to her feet, using the stump beside her to steady her step. "We came upon a hunter last night and I earned this lump."

"And your hand, and that bruise?"

Embarrassed by her lack of skill, Bylyn covered the injuries. "I'm ashamed to admit I am not very good with a bow."

Rasa raised an eyebrow, not surprised that the little sprite had embellished the truth about her fighting skills. "And Isolde?" she asked as she tugged on her boots.

Bylyn stretched, trying to force the cramps from her neck and shoulders. She didn't recall much, between the lump on her head and the sounds of the hunter's body being devoured by an angry wolf pack after, but Rasabel would never know. "It took all I had to defend her."

"Did it?" Rasa was skeptical but wanted to hear the story.

"Your sword gets very heavy in a long fight, and my arm was injured from the bow."

Rasa drew the weapon from the scabbard, inspecting the edge, before returning it to the saddlebag pile. "It can be heavy if you are untrained." She pulled the bow from the tree limb perch, nocked an arrow and fired it into the tree ten yards away. Her gear was not damaged, but she expected as much knowing Isolde would protect Bylyn. She admired the new sinew wrap around the fletching as she retrieved the arrow. Isolde's skills were still strong. "How did you get your head wound?" Rasa asked.

"It was the wolf," Bylyn said.

Rasa's head snapped up. *Is this why I woke up covered in blood?* she thought.

"It jumped as I was firing." Bylyn drew a pretend bow, reenacting the fight. "I was protecting your wife. I drew your sword and the hunter attacked me. Don't worry, your blade made a killing blow before I went down."

"Our hero," Rasabel teased.

"It isn't a matter of jest. Up close, the wolf is the biggest I've ever seen and that hunter had more than a dozen skins. Without my sword handling, he would have killed the wolf, for sure."

"Sword handling?" Rasa ran her hand along the horse's side, checking for debris in the mare's coat, readying for a saddle. It was laughable the way Bylyn spun an epic tale that excluded the true sword handler of their moonlit fight. "How is it you can handle a sword but not a bow?"

"I am a thief, not a hunter. A sword is like a stick. If I can swing it, I can fight." Bylyn stabbed and waved her arms, imitating a sword fight. "But a bow costs more than I have ever had and they are very difficult to come by."

"To come by," Rasabel mocked. "You mean they are hard to steal."

"If you want to put it that way, I suppose it is accurate."

Rasa didn't put the saddle or her bags on Onyx; instead she looped the quiver around the belt on her hip. "Let me show you something." She dug through the belongings until she found the wrap at the bottom of her bag. The gray leather wrap was adorned with intricate loops and rings similar to the detail on her cloak. "Cover your bruises with this."

"I have never worn—"

Rasa interrupted her. "It is a bracer," she explained, "and every archer should wear one."

"Does this one belong to her?" Bylyn asked, knowing it was too small to fit around Rasa's muscular forearm.

Rasa nodded. "It does."

Bylyn slid the cuff over her hand until her injury was protected. "It's a little big." She twisted her wrist and the leather spun around.

Rasa dropped the bow over her head and across her chest. "You do try my patience, Little Sprite."

Bylyn smiled at the affection in Rasa's words as the warrior cinched the lengths of lacing until they were snug enough to protect her from further bowstring injury.

"Are we having an adventure?" Bylyn asked.

Rasa held the girl by the bracer and dragged her to the edge of the forest. "We are having a lesson."

"You're going to teach me to use a weapon I will never own?" Bylyn jested.

"Yes." Rasa positioned herself behind the girl. "Stand up straight."

Bylyn made her best attempt and Rasa gave her a little shove. "Hey!"

Rasa chuckled. "Everything you do with a bow requires alignment."

Bylyn frowned. "What does that mean?" she asked.

Rasa nocked the arrow and drew the bow to her cheek. "Look at my body."

Bylyn swallowed hard, practically gulping as she admired the flex of Rasa's forearm, the bicep's swell and the unwavering stance the woman held. "Yes, I see."

Rasabel turned to look at her, noticing a bright blush to her cheeks. She did not wish to embarrass her little sprite, so she continued. "Look at my arm, and follow the arrow to the bow."

"Yes, I see it." Bylyn affirmed she was following. In fairness, she was also distracted. They'd traveled together for days. She'd seen the woman naked almost as much as she'd seen her clothed, but if she was truthful for once in her eighteen years, Rasabel was extraordinary with this bow tightening her body as much as the string.

"If you want your arrow to fly straight, you have to loose it that way." Rasa did not release the arrow, but let the bow return to form. "Now you try."

She handed it to Bylyn and the girl did her best to imitate the positions. She nocked an arrow and struggled to draw it to her cheek. "You make this look easy," Bylyn said.

"This bow was made for Isolde," Rasa explained. "The draw weight is too light for me but with a little practice, you could manage." She directed Bylyn's hands, separating her fingers on the bowstring to guide her grip. "Raise it to draw, but use these fingers."

Bylyn drew the bow. "That's not as hard."

"Exactly," Rasa said. "Do you feel the way your arm creates a line across your body from your bow to your nose?"

Bylyn could not hold the arrow any longer and released it, missing the target tree completely. "I guess not."

Rasa took the bow. "Watch closely," she instructed again, nocking the arrow against the string, drawing it to her cheek but holding it steady. "Look at my position. As I stand ready to shoot you can see my straight posture. You can't be wriggly like a worm; you have to be in line. The real trick to hitting your target is teaching your fingers to release in a way you can repeat. If you can do it a hundred times in practice, you can do it once with urgency."

"That's the real trick?" Bylyn chuckled.

"Watch again, but from this side so you can see what I mean."

Bylyn stepped around, studying every move. Rasa's fingers hooked the bowstring, her shoulder taut with control and her forearm flexing as she drew the arrow's fletching to her cheek. She inhaled, and on the release of breath the string slipped free.

Bylyn froze, thinking about the morning before, remembering the frantic climb to the top of the tower and Isolde's flip over the edge. Her forehead broke with sweat as she watched the woman slip, little by little, from her hand. She fought the well of tears.

"It is like losing grip instead of letting go," Rasa explained without understanding Bylyn's sudden emotion.

"I think I understand." Bylyn wiped her eyes.

"Good," Rasa said. Aware of the girl's discomfort, she asked, "Are you alright, Little Sprite?"

"I am. I was only thinking this would have been good information last night."

"Yes, it probably would," Rasa agreed. "Now, you try."

They shot every arrow in the quiver for hours until Bylyn felt comfortable. Rasa corrected the stance, tilting and adjusting Bylyn's body until the girl formed a solid and consistent position.

"How do you feel?" Rasa asked.

Bylyn steadied the quiver against her hip. "I feel better."

"Good. Now switch your hand holds."

Bylyn shook her head. "We aren't meant to use our left hands," she whispered. "It's not good luck."

"I am cursed in this life already. What more should I fear?" Rasa laughed as she stripped the bow from the girl and adjusted to shoot with her left hand. "I have learned to do everything with both hands. If you are wounded worse than you are now"—she pointed at Bylyn's injury with the tip of the arrow—"and if you cannot draw or hold as you have trained, luck will not save you, but switching hands might." She released the arrow, burying it in the tree. "This may be what separates you from life or death."

"Oh," Bylyn gasped. "But what if I can barely hit with my right hand?"

"If you can wound an attacker, you'll slow him down and give yourself time to retreat." Rasa gave the bow to Bylyn. "Sometimes it is okay to run."

"Can I run now?" Bylyn joked, worried the wrath of bad luck would follow if she repositioned with the weaker hand.

"There will be no running from our lesson if you intend to protect our Isolde."

Our Isolde, Bylyn thought but dared not repeat aloud. It was the first real and true time she'd felt part of something, part of someone and their life. She would stay. She would listen and she would learn to be better.

Rasa nudged her. "Try."

Bylyn reversed her grip. "It feels very uncomfortable." She nocked the arrow and drew it to her cheek. Her fingertips loosed the arrow and it struck the tree. "I hit it." She skipped in a circle.

"Do not celebrate just yet. When you can do that over and over, then we will dance."

Bylyn smiled. "I cannot imagine you dancing." She nocked a fresh arrow.

Rasa leaned against the tree behind her, watching the girl steady to shoot again. "I do quite a few things, or at least I did." She paused. "A lot has happened, and there are many challenges getting in the way of celebrating."

"Yes, it is a challenge to find celebration when you are hungry and alone," Bylyn said, not intending to voice her thoughts aloud.

"I have made the best of lonely days," Rasa said.

Bylyn patted her stomach. "And you are very good at filling a belly."

"It is a necessary chore, and hunting keeps my skills sharp," Rasa shared.

Bylyn had witnessed the warrior's skills firsthand and did not worry for her sharpness, but she felt the warrior's mood shift and wondered if asking about hunting would be welcomed. "Might I ask you a question?"

Rasa smiled. "You might."

"We have been together these few days and it got me thinking." Bylyn hesitated. "Wondering, really."

"Go ahead," Rasa encouraged. "What were you wondering?"

"It's a curious thing really. You are a warrior, there is no denying this truth, but why is it you hunt for a bird of prey? Aren't they—"

"For Isolde," the warrior interrupted, correcting her. "I hunt for Isolde. She is my wife, my everything, and although she will not remember the days, she will know when she comes to camp at night that I think of her."

"She knows." Bylyn shot an arrow, splintering the bark she was aiming for. "Her adoration and appreciation are impossible to hide. Just as yours is, too."

"That is love, Little Sprite."

Love, Bylyn thought. Yes, there was love between Isolde and Rasabel, a love large enough to survive two long and lonely years. A love any one would suffer for, but what if the suffering could end? What if the curse separating the two could be broken? Seizing the moment, Bylyn mentioned the priest's plan. "Have you considered Father Intan's vision about altering the curse?"

Rasa's stance stiffened.

"He says there could be a way to break—"

Rasa held up her hand. "We will not speak of him."

"But what if?"

"Bylyn, I can no longer trust anything he says." Rasa's icy stare accented with a deep frown left no room for negotiation. "You have to understand why there is no trust between us."

Bylyn nodded. "I do understand, but that doesn't change what he says will happen."

"You should practice." Rasa tapped the full quiver. "I'm going to take Onyx for a drink."

Rasa disappeared long enough for Bylyn to shoot her arrows a few times. When she returned to camp, the little sprite was cursing her bad luck.

"Such language," Rasa jested as she tethered the horse to the bush.

"I have lost a second arrow, and I..." It was clear Bylyn was distraught.

"I lose them too," Rasa admitted. "Tomorrow we learn how to replace that which was lost."

"I've never done that either," Bylyn said. "You think a bow is hard to acquire—arrows are even trickier, unless they end up in you."

"I have experience with that." Rasa patted her leg, where a terrible wound should have been. The hawk circled above them. "As does Isolde."

Bylyn studied the pair, intrigued by the way Rasabel admired the hawk. It was a terrible curse to be a part of.

"Are you ready to use those skills out there?" Rasa pointed at the prairie grasses.

Bylyn took her time, wrestling with the idea of saying no and slowing down their travels. Intan hadn't shown up last night, and if the plan to confront the bishop were to come to fruition, the old man needed to catch up to them. "Can I wash first? I have worked hard today."

"You can wash in a few hours when we get to camp," Rasa insisted. "After traveling to save Isolde, we are very far from Acadia. We can't waste any more time."

"What's one more day?"

"Are you dragging your feet, Little Sprite?"

Bylyn flopped the boots onto her feet. "Yes, but not on purpose. If you had to wear these, you'd be dragging too."

Rasa slid down the saddle. "Why don't you ride today?" She didn't give Bylyn a chance to refuse as she hoisted the girl up.

"How is this faster?"

Rasa kept pace with the trotting horse. "It isn't."

Bylyn was confused by the woman running alongside them. She was serious most of the time but when she wasn't it threw their relationship off balance. She considered   the idea of a friend—about what it meant to have and to be one. She couldn't remember any person ever helping her the way Rasabel and Isolde did.

"Thank you," Bylyn said.

"You are welcome, Little Sprite."

CHAPTER SEVENTEEN

Isolde had no memory of her day or of the moment when her animal self became human, but she was unsettled in a way she hadn't been for two years. She understood her new travel companion was now a part of her cursed life. The addition filled the loneliness of her dark nights, but she envied the lost days and the moments the girl spent with Rasabel.

It felt like a betrayal to find comfort in companionship when what she wanted was a single touch from her wife. Stripped of everything, in these naked moments, she could not escape the truth; she was existing, not living. Her marriage was painfully solitary. But the need for intimacy was the most excruciating of all as Rasa's touch faded into memory.

Bylyn was asleep when Isolde came into camp and the moon lit a path as she stepped around the sleeping girl. She saw the bump on Bylyn's temple and shook her head, knowing Rasa would have addressed the girl's lack of fighting ability. Rasa's teaching skills brought a smile to Isolde, even if she knew what a terrible fighter the girl was.

"Don't worry, love," Isolde whispered to the darkness. "I remember everything you taught me and I'll teach all of it to her." She dropped the shirt over her head. "I'll take care of her."

She didn't have siblings, and this was true for her wife too, but Isolde felt a sisterly bond forming between herself and Bylyn.

Bylyn stirred. "You have found me," she grumbled, still half asleep.

"You have been found." She unfolded the cloak and wrapped herself inside it. "How is your head?" she asked.

"This?" Bylyn touched the lump and regretted it immediately. "A little tender, but Rasa says I will survive."

Isolde chuckled. "She would know. She's very good at surviving."

Sensing Isolde's melancholy, Bylyn made a quick decision. "She had some words to say. She wanted me to share them with you."

Isolde turned, giving away her desperate need for any word from Rasa, and wishing to the goddess that the words were coming from Rasa and not the girl. "Did she?"

"I swear." Bylyn touched her hand to her heart.

Isolde was skeptical but appreciated the effort Bylyn put into comforting her. "And what were these words?"

"Well, she was angry when she saw my wounds."

"She is never forgiving of injuries," Isolde said, "but I'm sure by now you've seen she has scars of her own."

Bylyn could not hide the blush. "Our captain has many. They are hard to miss when she arrives as you do after the transformation."

"Yes, after." Isolde flattened her palm against her breast. She too had scars left behind from living in the wild with this terrible curse. "And what was her assessment of your wounds?"

"She scolded me"—Bylyn wrinkled her nose—"and after the scolding she forced a bow into my hand and gave me a lesson, all the while saying, 'You must learn to fight and stay strong.'" Bylyn tipped side-to-side, mimicking the warrior. "'Isolde is everything to my heart, and the only hope for my future, and you will be her protector.'"

Isolde knew many things about Rasabel that would never change. They were true to each other, heart and soul, but her wife knew Isolde possessed the skills to protect herself. "She did not say that."

Bylyn raised her hand. "I swear."

Isolde shook her head. "You should not swear such things when they aren't true."

"I have traveled with the woman for days now," Bylyn said. "I think I know her fairly well, and if there is one thing she is consumed by, it is her love for you."

"I wouldn't argue that, but she taught me to fight, as she teaches you, and protection is not what I require." Isolde's expression was stern.

Bylyn felt the scolding in Isolde's glare, and was certain it was how a caring mother's reprimand would feel. "What I meant—"

Isolde held up a finger, silencing Bylyn. "I know what you meant."

"I only meant that I spent all day with your bow." Bylyn mimicked pulling a bowstring. "Rasa said I am no longer a threat to you or myself."

"Good." Isolde forced a smile. "So the future hangs one less shadow over us."

It wasn't an inspiring compliment, nor a half-hearted pat on the back, but Bylyn felt accomplished in her new skill. "Perhaps—"

"We cannot manage another curse," Isolde interrupted, her thoughts clouded by Bylyn's lessons with Rasa.

"Another curse?" Bylyn saw her sorrow. "What is it?"

Isolde sighed. "I have often wondered if our love was the real curse." She tossed a chunk of wood at the fire.

"This is not true," Bylyn said.

"From the moment we said forever, we have been under this cloud of darkness." Isolde shared. Tonight was the first in a long time that she felt adrift. Her longing for Rasa seemed unbearable as she listened to the girl spin this tale about the life she and Rasabel were having without her. She patted the girl's leg. "Come on, let me teach you how to use my favorite weapon."

"Is it a sword?" Bylyn asked.

Isolde shook her head. "It is so much better." She opened her hand, revealing the sling she cherished. "All you will ever need is one good arm and a few stones."

Bylyn followed her teacher to the edge of camp. "It is a little dark for rock fighting."

"As you learned last night, trouble comes calling at any time of day." She picked up a stone and tucked it in the leather pocket of her sling. There was no hesitation as Isolde's arm rotated, twirling the rock-filled pocket at her side and releasing the stone to strike the tree.

Bylyn wondered if the trees feared this couple as they practiced their weapon skills. "Perhaps a sling is easier than a bow?" Bylyn suggested.

Isolde shook her head. "Place this over your finger." She positioned the loop to fit in Bylyn's hand. "Tuck the rock in and repeat my movements."

Bylyn pointed at the tree. "Would you like me to hit the same target?"

Isolde chuckled. "We will work up to hitting a target."

"Work up?" She began twirling the string, whipping it around. Isolde covered her head as she ducked to the ground. She knew what was coming, understood exactly how overconfident Bylyn would be.

Bylyn released the stone straight up into the sky, "I see." She had no time to run or duck as the stone landed near her floppy-booted foot. "This is not as easy."

Isolde chuckled as she took the weapon from her hand. "Perhaps we should let Rasa teach you during the day."

"It might be less dangerous." Bylyn agreed.

"Not less dangerous," Isolde said as she folded the sling into the pouch on her belt. "Only smarter."

"Your wife is a very good teacher." Bylyn said, not intending to break the lighthearted mood.

Isolde sat to warm herself by the fire. "My wife is very good at a great many things."

The firelight reflected off Isolde's face and the sadness hurt Bylyn's heart. She needed to talk about the curse, and needed to warn her of the priest's plan to end it. "There is something I want to share with you."

Isolde turned, wiping the tear from her cheek. "What is it, Bylyn?"

The sound of horse's hooves on trampled ground interrupted the conversation. Bylyn was almost as quick to her feet as Isolde.

"Whoa." Intan coughed and the mule-sized animal stopped. Intan rolled off the cart, and with the aid of a crooked stick he stumbled into their camp. He was as unwashed as he was in the crumbling castle. His arrival was providential as Bylyn wondered how to explain a plan she didn't quite understand.

"What are you doing here?" Bylyn jumped up, doing a terrible job of pretending not to know why he was there.

Short of breath, he squatted beside them. "Sit down, girl. I'm not chasing after you." He leaned toward Isolde, knowing he was unwelcome but understanding the risk.

"Have you come chasing after me?" Isolde asked.

The fire felt warm in the cool night air and he let the heat settle the chill. "I have."

Looking upon his face felt like a betrayal to her wife, and his presence multiplied her pain. "I'm grateful for this." Isolde patted her breast, a healed scar where the wound should be. "I don't know how to repay that kindness, but Rasa would never—"

"Rasa has vowed to kill the bishop," Intan interrupted. There was no time to waste as he blurted the ill-conceived plan.

Isolde gasped. "What do you mean?" After years of living in forests and fields she didn't recognize as home, appearing in the ruins where Intan lived was an unwelcome surprise. Rasa's revenge was what she feared most when the architecture of Acadia's territory became familiar.

"She told me only a day ago," he said, "that she means to kill the bishop with that sword. Run it straight through his heart with no care about what will follow." Intan's hands trembled, and he stumbled to the cart, returning with a jug of wine. He unstopped the cork and poured a steadying gulp in his mouth. "Surely that will make the curse last forever."

"The curse *is* forever," Isolde said, walking away from the smell of his wine-soaked breath.

Bylyn studied Isolde in the moonlight, truly looking upon her as she did Rasa. The language of their bodies was so similar she wondered if they were twin siblings and not wives. Isolde leaned against the tree, one arm crossed over her chest and the other fisted for a fight. She was always ready—for what, Bylyn did not know—but it was clear that neither of the women ever truly found rest.

"But what if the curse is not forever?" Intan drank again, this time taking in twice as much. "I have been told there is a chance to fix what's broken." His tone was desperate, pleading for her to let her defenses down.

"To fix what *you* have broken." Isolde pounded her chest. "Do you understand what you have done to me, what you have done to us?"

His wine jug tilted toward the dirt. "And I have cursed my own life every day since."

Isolde snatched the wine. "You've lost yourself in drink, Intan. I've lost myself to the shadows and —" The wolf's howl interrupted her, and they all turned toward the sound. "And I've lost her."

The fire crackled. It was the only sound, as Intan didn't know what to say and Isolde feared what she might say next.

Bylyn drew the courage to speak. "You should listen to what he has to share." She stood, finding the determination to put herself between them. "If there is hope for you and Rasa to be together, wouldn't it be worth the chance?"

"It is impossible." Isolde tossed a log at the fire. "The bishop made a deal with something so dark I could never understand it."

"But I do," Intan said, abandoning his drink. He returned to the cart. "I have seen it."

"What have you seen?" Isolde stood closer to his unkempt body. "Have you seen a confessor?"

He fell to his knees, hands clasped, as he begged her to hear. "I have seen a day forthcoming. A night when she will not howl, and a day where you will not fly."

Isolde looked down at him, taking in the pathetic presence of a tired old man. "There is no such thing, you fool."

"What if there is?" Bylyn interrupted. "What if Intan's salvation is to bring this news to you? What if the dark forces the Bishop commands can be defeated by the dreams of this drunken bit of a man? But more importantly, what if the goddess has heard your crying in the night and this is the answer to every tear?"

Isolde was fearful of feeling hope again. "And if it is not true?"

"Then you are no worse than you are right now." Bylyn picked up the sword. "Would you dare to miss this chance, a chance to hold the love of your life forever?"

"There is not one thing I would desire more." Isolde closed her eyes, hearing the solemn howl of her wolf. "Not one."

"You should listen to what he has to say and we should make our own plan."

~~~~~~~~~~

"This is a terrible plan," Intan said from the bottom of a muddy pit.

Bylyn stabbed the ground with Rasa's sword, busting the soil into pieces they could remove. Their hole was nearly deep enough to capture the dark animal.

Isolde had gone into the forest to lure the wolf to camp. It felt like a betrayal to bring the animal back and capture her, but it was their only way to convince Rasabel not to kill the bishop.

"It's the best plan we have," Bylyn said.

"What will it do to trap her down here?" Intan grumbled.

"Isolde knows better than anyone what they need," Bylyn said as she tossed the sword out of the hole. She was agile enough to pull herself up but Intan was not.

"Help me out, girl," he huffed, and Bylyn dropped back in to push the man from below.

"You need less drinking and more walking," she grunted as Intan kicked her shoulder and hefted himself out.

"When you're as old as I am, we will talk; until then, do not judge."

Isolde moved from the shadow, her hand light against the dark fur of the wolf at her hip. The animal was large up
~~~~~~~~~~

close, and as they neared, a deep growl echoed from the beast.

"Get out of the hole." Isolde's whisper was panicked. There was no way her wolf would move forward into a trap.

Bylyn's head popped up from below, startling the wolf. On instinct, to protect Isolde, the animal leapt toward Bylyn, knocking them into the pit together. The animal's weight was impossible to move as Bylyn fought to escape. The wolf scratched and snarled as Bylyn flailed, her hands and feet desperate to kick the beast away.

Isolde jumped in, wrapping herself around the wolf, using every close-contact tactic she could to save Bylyn from death.

Ultimately it was her voice, the soothing sounds of love, that lured nearly everyone to listen. "Bel, my love," she whispered against the animal's ear and it was like the world stopped and no creatures existed but Isolde and the wolf who loved her. "Get her out," Isolde commanded Intan as she wrapped the animal with her in the cloak.

"Give me your hand, Bylyn," Intan said as he laid on his belly beside the pit.

A bloodstained hand reached up. Bylyn could not catch her breath or think as her heart pounded in her head, and her body vibrated with the rush to survive. Only with Intan's help could she kick her way out of the ground. It was the one instance Bylyn did not mind being so close to the old priest. "Thank you, Father," she huffed. "I feared I would not survive."

Isolde felt the coldness of the earth as she held the animal to her body. Her chest heaved, gasping to calm herself and desperate to keep her wolf beside her in the ground. It felt like a grave, like this would be the last place the two would ever be together. She didn't fight the tears as she rested against the damp earth.

"This curse," Isolde whispered. "Damn this curse."

~~~~~~~~~~

After years of sunrises and sunsets, Isolde knew when the transformation was coming. She and her wolf lay on the floor of the pit, the thick fur of the animal's neck soft in her hand, the cloak holding them close. Isolde felt the moon's brightness fade as the light of day took hold. The energy of the curse's power vibrated in her skin, twisting skin and bone from human to something she had no awareness of.

The fur in her hand evolved into flesh, hard muscle where bristly hair had been. It happened in seconds, this passing from beast to woman, and Isolde looked into the eyes she had not seen in forever. The change was a bright burst of light to dark, dark to light, half a heartbeat, not a single breath, before Rasa was there and Isolde was no more than a feathered animal taking flight.

The bird squawked as her wings opened and she flew from the pit.

Rasa's aching howl transformed into a tortured and desperate scream.

Bylyn covered her ears, masking the sounds of suffering created by trapping this woman in a twisted reality.

Rasa scrambled out of the hole, as if somehow she could fly away with the creature that left her behind. She clawed at the loose soil, screaming for her love. "Isolde!"
~~~~~~~~~~

She climbed from the pit, her eyes black as night and out of control.

Intan and Bylyn were not prepared for the storm that followed. Rasa's manner transformed from sorrow to embarrassment, and then to rage.

"What have you done?" Naked from head to toe, her hands clenched in fists to fight, she grabbed Intan by the throat.

"You needed to see."

"As if I haven't watched for two years!" she screamed, tossing the man like he had no bones. Intan did not fight her rage; in fact, he expected it, and some part of him wished she'd end him right now and take his shame away.

"Rasa." Bylyn grabbed her shoulder.

The warrior dropped the man and spun to take the girl to task. "You." Rage fueled her reaction as she grabbed the girl. "You have no idea what you've done."

Bylyn closed her eyes as Rasa raised a fist to strike her. The stillness made little sense as Bylyn felt a drop on her face. There was another, and then another, until her body shook—not from punches but from the tremble of Rasabel's tears.

"M'lady," Bylyn whispered.

Rasa steadied the girl on her feet before collapsing to the ground. It was all too much for her to understand: the split-second sight of Isolde, her eyes, her lips, after countless days trying to remember, it was overwhelming to take it all in.

"Rasa," Bylyn called her again, but weeping overtook the warrior. Bylyn curled around the trembling soul, offering nothing more than understanding as she witnessed years of unresolved emotions.

Rasa pushed her away. "No." It felt like betrayal to find comfort in another's arms. "No," she said again before running from camp. She didn't stop until she heard the rush of the river. Her body was covered in dirt and, without thinking, she fell into the current. It would be so easy to go under and never come to the surface, but she had seen her. She had looked upon the love she needed more than breath and suddenly the image was more than a memory.

"Her hair is long, like mine." Rasa relived that split-second glimpse. "And her eyes, they are still hers, and I can see I am still there in her heart." Tears fell as the dirt transformed to muddy smears before disappearing in the water. How could Intan and Bylyn not understand how cruel this trapping was to her soul?

She sank beneath the water again, this time letting the current carry her downstream. It was too much.

CHAPTER EIGHTEEN

Bylyn lay against the mossy ground, ignoring the light of day as she tried to recover from the wounds the wolf had made to her chest and shoulders. Her skin burned and her body trembled as flashes between hot and cold confused her senses. This curse was taking a toll on her, too.

Rasa returned to camp naked and covered in sweat. She dropped two freshly-skinned animals near the fire and stared at Bylyn. The little sprite shivered beneath the fabric, her discomfort obvious as she curled herself in the cloak Rasa treasured—the rag she shared with Isolde alone before meeting this little thief.

Rasa disregarded thoughts of betrayal. It was clear from the scattering of dirt and the stains of mud on their faces that the evening's events stretched far beyond the momentary appearance of Isolde in the pit. Rasa had felt a range of emotions as she hunted, fighting rage and frustration as she tried to add to her memory the brief glimpse of Isolde.

The priest was in her camp. The gutless coward was here, and what little peace she had found as she hunted disappeared at the sight of her betrayer.

"What did you do to me last night?" Rasa accused.

Intan's answer was sharp. "We tried to prevent you from killing us." He was working hard to refill the hole they'd dug to capture the wolf, pushing the piles of dirt with the bottom of his boot.

"Killing *you*?" she questioned. "Why would I kill you?"

He grunted. "You truly have no memory of your other half life?"

Rasa placed a log on the fire to bring the flames high enough for cooking. "I have no memories of my nights, very much like she has no memories of her days." Her tone softened as her focus turned to the gliding hawk. It was impossible to look away; she was enchanted by the carefree glide of the bird circling above them. "Tell me what happened here."

"We tried to capture you last night," he said.

Rasa's attention snapped to his words. It was clear this was an emotional ambush. Her hand trembled with rage as she sliced meat from the raw rabbit, before forcing the roasting skewer through the animal's carcass. "So, it is done." She paused to hold the sliver of meat and the hawk swooped down, grasping the food and landing on the saddle to eat it. "You have shared your convoluted story of absolution with Isolde?"

It was sobering to watch the bird devour her meal while the man who betrayed them sat warming himself by their camp fire. "It is not a convoluted story, and yes, she agrees we should wait and confront the Bishop united."

"We!" Rasa yelled, no longer able to contain her rage-fueled emotions. "You saw our *we* in the pit you're shoveling to fill." She stepped closer to Intan, towering over the man as he scrambled to stand. "There is no *we* anymore unless *we* keep our eyes open for a split second as the sun rises and the moon sleeps." She tipped her dagger, pointing at Intan's chest. "There has not been a *we* in two years and no dream from an old drunken man can undo it."

"I believe it can." Bylyn groaned and was slow to sit. "Isolde believes it too or she wouldn't have helped us last night and you wouldn't have seen her in the breaking of dawn this morning."

"Have you been sipping his wine, too?" Rasa's tone was biting.

Bylyn stood, the heaviness of the cloak's weight keeping her in place. "I saw you, Rasa. As much as you hide behind the brute force of your skills and honor, I saw your love for her."

"Love is not enough." Rasa stabbed the dagger into its sheath. "Not anymore."

Bylyn steadied herself against the tree, feeling the pain of her wounds and no longer able to bear the weight of the cloak. She did not need physical strength to say her next words. "You… are… a… coward!"

Intan's gasp was loud.

Bylyn thought she understood the skills Rasabel possessed until the warrior leapt to her feet with a fist knotted to strike. The calloused hand clutched Bylyn's shirt collar and the girl almost fainted from the masterful maneuver.

"I have been called many things, by many people, Little Sprite"—she shook Bylyn—"but I have never been called a coward."

"And yet here you are"—Bylyn choked out the next words—"ignoring what is possible, and cursing her to a life without you in it." Bylyn's toes were the only thing touching the ground as Rasabel stood to her full height. "That's what a coward would do."

Rasa tossed the girl to the ground. "You have no idea what you are talking about. The torture I have lived these two years."

The wounds on Bylyn's chest and shoulders opened and blood seeped through the thin fabric of her shirt.

"What have you done to her?" Intan crawled close to the girl, cradling her across his lap.

"What have *I* done?" Rasa was confused and stepped back, stunned by the sight of the girl's injury.

"Yes, you." Intan unlaced Bylyn's shirt, revealing the bright red blood seeping from the marks on her chest.

"She is wounded?" Rasa didn't move as Intan's accusation hit. In battle, blood ran and the wounds of war made sense. But this was a girl, not a warrior, wearing wounds Rasa did not understand. "Who attacked her?"

Bylyn looked at Intan, begging with her eyes for him to remain silent. Yes, Rasa caused her wounds, but she was not responsible for the actions of an animal desperate to survive.

Intan looked at Rasabel. "You. You did this to her."

Rasa steadied herself against the tree beside her, sliding down, feeling the bark claw against her skin as two years of carefully-constructed survival came ripping apart.

~~~~~~~~~~

Hours later, the warrior sat still as if frozen like ice in a winter storm. The reality of their plan to capture the wolf had left her catatonic, and Bylyn found the reaction more frightening than anything before.

"She has not moved," Bylyn said, resting a safe distance from the silent warrior. Enough time had passed that Intan had redressed her wounds, and the rabbit was fully cooked.

"She will move when she is ready," Intan said.

"She stares at her hands like a statue in a cathedral." Bylyn felt the ease of pain as the tingling sensation from the salve began to work.

"Give her some peace. She has spent a very long time alone," Intan explained. "Let her have a chance to understand what we've done."

"Do we have time for that?" Bylyn asked, feeling the weight of Intan's prophecy hanging over them.

"We don't have a choice, girl. She needs to sort it all in her head."

"Is she dreaming in there?" Bylyn waved a hand in front of the warrior's shadowy staring face.

"Let's leave her be." Intan pushed the girl away from camp. "Let her have whatever brings her to our side."

~~~~~~~~~~

"There is no time," Rasa held Isolde's hands to her chest, trying to control her lover's wandering fingers.

"What do I care about time?" Isolde's body thrust forward, pushing her lover against the armory wall.

"Is, we must care until we are away from Acadia." Rasa's attempt to push back was met with unanticipated dominance. "You have become quite strong, my love."

Isolde raised her eyebrow. "You are a very good teacher." She untangled their hands enough to separate the laces of Rasa's shirt. "I can fight any foe, much like you do."

Rasa didn't want to fight against Isolde; she only wanted to fight for her. "I see you have a strategy."

"I have a wicked plan to relieve you of this shirt and those trousers." Isolde's smile punctuated the sentence as her mouth found the taut length of Rasa's neck.

"This was not a technique I brought for you." Rasa's head fell against the wall as Isolde's lips trailed down and her tongue licked the muscled curve of her chest.

"You must trust that I can lead you to our future with some of my own techniques."

Rasa gasped as Isolde's mouth found her breast. "Where you go—" Her hands *slapped the wall, grasping to steady her weakening legs.*

Isolde paused, a deliciously wicked smile forming as she questioned, "Where you go?"

"Oh, goddess." Rasa's breath hitched as she repeated, "Wherever you go, I will follow… always, I will follow."

Isolde tore at the shirt's hem, raising it up and over her lover's head, trapping Rasa's hands above her. "In the future, when you are stubborn, I will remind you of this surrender."

"Perhaps I will be stubborn a lot."

"Isolde." Rasa's whispered cry fell against the icy ground. Dreaming of the past hurt. Awareness of a solitary life hurt. Being alive without Isolde was more pain than she could bear.

~~~~~~~~~~~

Rasabel was curled in a ball on the ground when Intan and Bylyn returned to camp. Bylyn carried the sword, while Intan dropped the chopped tree limbs beside the fire. The hawk sat on the horn of the saddle, watching everything as though she could protect the sleeping and otherwise defenseless warrior.

Bylyn didn't like the silence. "Can you hunt, Intan?"

He chuckled. "I can set a trap and I am still pretty good with a bow. If I'd thought to bring mine."

"She'll need to eat when she wakes."
~~~~~~~~~~~

"She can hunt, and she can fight," Rasa interrupted. "She can also hear everything you're saying."

"You have returned to the living," Intan said.

Rasabel pushed herself upright. "I have no idea how to return to anything."

"What does that mean?" Bylyn asked.

"You have done something to me, Little Sprite." Rasa stood and brushed the dirt from her body. "I have spoken to the gods, to the goddesses, and everything in between. For two years I have bargained, leveraging my very life to share one word with Isolde again, for a single chance to look into her eyes so she could see that my love for her is still there." She wiped at the tear on her cheek. "Three days ago, I heard the bells of Acadia chiming and I could not guess why the guards were summoned on high alert. I suppose I was called in a way I have never been before, but I wasn't expecting to find you."

"I'm not exactly salvation." Bylyn shrugged and winced as the gesture flexed her wounds.

"You don't understand… you were… you are." Rasa looked at Intan, stepping close enough to strike him down. "We are trapped together in this curse we did not choose. But I see it now. I understand that you came back to us." She held out a hand and the bird leapt onto it. "I understand what she was doing last night." She stroked the bird's breast. "She knows me so well that she planned for my stubbornness."

"What are you saying?" Bylyn asked. "She sounds mad, Intan."

"I'm not mad. I am awake, and for the first time in two years I am not alone in the fight against this curse." Rasa stepped to where the saddle lay on the ground, setting the bird on the horn. She rummaged through her belongings for her shirt and pants before hastily pulling on her boots. "There is work to do."

"Slow down." Intan grabbed her shoulders, spinning her to face him. "We are not inside your head."

"It's probably a good thing right now." Rasa chuckled, staring back at him. "I have a plan."

"Is it better than a hole in the ground?" Bylyn asked. "Because her talons are as sharp as your claws, and my chest may be small, but it cannot withstand another attack."

"There will be no digging, Little Sprite." Rasa sidestepped the horse. "We will fasten a cage strong enough to hold a wolf."

"Can we fasten a cage to hold two?" Bylyn held up her first and second fingers, and Intan chuckled.

"Two?" Rasa questioned.

"I fear to say this, but you are a very well-made wolf."

Rasa's brow furrowed. "Am I?"

Bylyn held up a third finger. "A cage for three wolves might be better."

Rasabel did not argue, knowing that the new plan hinged on trapping her animal form. "Let me teach you how to lash a cage that will hold three wolves."

~~~~~~~~~~

"They must be green." Rasa pushed against the saplings to test their strength. "If the limbs are dead, my wolf will surely snap them."
~~~~~~~~~~

Bylyn grinned, struck by how easily Rasa was referring to her alternate being. "This one?" She measured its thickness alongside the girth of her wrist.

"Good," Rasa said. "Ten more just like it."

"Great." Bylyn rolled her eyes. "Ten more." She hadn't worked this hard in almost as many years as the curse they were trying to break.

They dragged the limbs into camp and found Intan perched on a log, twisting layers of fibrous plant stalks to make lengths of cordage to fasten the cage together. The pile bundled around his feet was impressive.

"That's good work." Bylyn inspected it. "Very good work."

"You can take your smart self over there and make a cage." The priest swatted at her and lost tension on his twist, causing his current cord to unravel. "Ah, look what you've made me do."

"Me?" Bylyn dropped her saplings on the ground.

He began twisting the fibers again. "Yes, you."

"The two of you squabble like old barn cats," Rasa interrupted.

"It is the pressure of doing all this hard work," Bylyn said. "I am a free spirit, you know."

"Take your free spirit over there and cut those limbs six lengths of your stolen boots," Rasa teased, imitating how the girl should step to measure each sapling limb.

"I'll have you know I liberated this fine pair of boots," Bylyn said.

"How is that so?" Rasa chuckled. She couldn't wait to hear this tale of liberation.

"If I hadn't come to find them when I did, they'd be having a terrible, dung-covered life."

"We can't have that for such fine footwear," Rasa teased.

Bylyn laid the limbs on the ground and scored each one after pacing six lengths of her boots. "That's exactly what I thought, too."

~~~~~~~~~~

Intan kicked the hot coals away from the fire so he could collect a pile of ash. He and Bylyn were finally able to appreciate the strategist Rasabel truly was as they focused on executing the new and improved plan.

"This feels wrong, Rasa," Bylyn said as she lashed the final section securing the cage around the warrior's body.

"Wrong because I'm naked inside here or because you're out there tying me in?" Rasa joked as she tugged one by one at every lash point to check their strength.

Bylyn thought about the question; there was a gorgeous muscled woman, one most would dream of, naked and tying herself into a cage with Bylyn's help. "Yes to everything you said."

Rasa chuckled as she reached through to grab a handful of the ash Intan was piling beside the cage. "This is the only way to sneak me into the bishop's palace." She smothered her face, believing if she tinted herself with white ash it would cling, making her animal form appear more gray than black.

"What if this doesn't work?" Bylyn placed a board across the back of the cart, locking the cage in place for the night's journey.

"If there is trouble, Isolde will know what to do."
~~~~~~~~~~

Bylyn smiled. "You have faith in her." It was a statement, not a question.

"I have never doubted she knows what to do in my absence. It's the only way we have survived these years apart. I have to trust that she, along with the two of you, can lead us to a different future."

"We will not let you down." Bylyn began covering the horse's tack with dirt and leaves, hidden behind the cage. Rasabel and Onyx would need the saddle tomorrow, along with the sword tucked beneath the thatched treelimb cell.

"I know you will not let me down," Rasa said as she waited for the sun to disappear in the horizon, surrendering to whatever the morning would bring.

CHAPTER NINETEEN

The man adjusted the wolf hide draped over his shoulders. The animal-skin cloak was too large for his frame and the wolf-head mask drooped down over his eyes, blocking his vision every time he shook his head. He was vying for the bounty offered for a black wolf's pelt, and wearing the mask of the great hunter Greybeck was his only way to that fortune.

It was like a gift from the gods when he heard the hungry pack in the woods, and even doubly good fortune when he followed the sound, finding the camp where the hunter's bounty lay. The imposter cinched his disguise tighter, hoping he would make it inside the bishop's castle and that one of the many wolf pelts piled in this stolen cart was the one the holy man demanded.

The guards were heavy around the gate, scrutinizing every cart and rider as they arrived.

"You cannot enter with that," the taller guard said as the man rolled the wagon to the checkpoint. He flipped the corner of the fabric covering the wolf pelts, believing wares for the morning's food market were underneath.

"Your lord bishop would disagree." The imposter sat forward, keeping the cloak in place to cover his face. "The bishop has summoned me and I have come." He tugged the tarp off his cart, revealing the furs under it.

The shorter guard whispered as he pointed his sword at the wolf-masked hunter. "See the headpiece? He is the one they call Greybeck."

"He is not the one," the tall guard answered. "He is an imposter."

"I am not," the man argued, but in truth he was an imposter, and if he was going to fool anyone with his disguise, he'd have to begin at this gate. The imposter was the only one who knew that the owner of this red-headed wolf garment had met a terrible fate the night before, but it would not end this way for him. "The bishop has called for wolf pelts," the hunter said, "and that is what I bring. Look through if you must, but I'm sure I have what your lord demands."

"Let him pass," the shorter guard said. "He is Greybeck. I saw that headpiece only days ago, and if anyone can please the bishop it will be his chosen hunter."

"That's right," the imposter said as he rode through. "I am the one they call Greybeck."

Word traveled quickly through the town as trappers waited for a chance to impress the bishop with their kills; Greybeck the great hunter had arrived. The lesser-skilled hunters made way for him to approach the castle. It was over for them. If Greybeck had a loaded cart, he was sure to deliver what the bishop demanded, and their chances at the bounty were gone as well.

~~~~~~~~~~

The bishop stabbed the carcass with the base of his staff. It was an unusual instrument, fitted with a sharp point for defense. The holy man liked the weight of his staff, and this hidden spear tip was perfect for damaging human flesh. He prodded another hide. "Where is Greybeck?" He scowled. "He would be the better hunter. I'm wasting my time with these fools."

"We have not heard from him, Lord Bishop," Captain Fleur said.

The bishop waved for the pile to be removed. "I grow tired, Fleur."

The captain wiped blood from the staff's spear before replacing the cover to hide the weapon. "I understand that word of your bounty has traveled the countryside. Every able-bodied person with a trap has arrived in Acadia with furs. It is impossible for all my guards to know your Greybeck." Fleur did not look into the bishop's eyes, knowing if he did the man's anger would be directed at him.

"These peasants ride in on their carts with dogs and anything covered with dark fur." The bishop wiped his hands on the back of Fleur's tunic. "Greybeck knows this countryside; he knows how to catch and kill."

"Yes, Lord Bishop."
~~~~~~~~~~

"No more. After tonight I want no more animals inside the palace until Greybeck brings the one I want."

A guard entered. "My lord, the hunter Greybeck has arrived."

The bishop smiled. "There, you see, Fleur. If you have faith, the good lord above will answer your prayers."

"Yes, Lord Bishop." It was absurd to believe the bishop prayed for such things, but he did. Fleur tipped his head as he backed away from the altar. It had been an afternoon of death parading through the gardens: pelts, whole carcasses and pieces of wolves he often gagged at seeing. The captain did not understand his lord's obsession or to what end he demanded such slaughter.

"Send my hunter in," the bishop commanded.

The imposter entered, slow to approach the bishop as the drag of his wolf-skin cloak weighed him down. Two guards followed behind the imposter, pushing the cart loaded with wolf pelts.

"The great hunter brings me many hides, but do you have the one I want?" The bishop pounded the floor with his staff and Fleur scurried to remove the spear-head covering.

One by one, the bishop skewered the pelts, transferring them into a pile on the chamber floor. "No," he said as each one failed his test. "No!"

"It must be here, Lord Bishop," the hunter said.

The bishop jerked his head to glare at the hunter. It was the submissive tone, the respect for authority, that drew the bishop's suspicion. This man was dressed like the great Greybeck, but he did not act or smell like the hunter he had challenged a few days before.

"You are not the one they call Greybeck!" The bishop's accusation was loud, echoing through the hall. He moved with grace, slow and intimidating as he towered over the imposter.

The hunter swallowed hard, stammering, "The one?" He knew from the evil in the bishop's glare that his disguise had failed.

The bishop stabbed the wolf-face mask covering the imposter's head. "You are not Greybeck." The pelt flew across the chamber, landing at the guards' feet.

"I am sorry, Lord Bishop. I only wished to bring you—"

"You wished to trick me." The bishop stabbed the man in the shoulder. "You wished to steal from my holy treasury and take what you did not earn."

Spittle flew at the imposter's unmasked face. Desperate to survive, he said, "I found the pelts, Lord Bishop. I confess. I thought what you were looking for might be among them."

The bishop glared, disgusted by the liar and thief. "You"—he stabbed the man over and over until he collapsed on the chamber floor—"thought wrong." The bishop wrinkled his nose as a pool of blood spread through the cracks between the tiles of the floor. This was not an efficient way to find the wolf.

"Clean up this mess, Fleur." The bishop waved as he exited the chamber. "I grow tired of this search. After the courtyard clears of hunters, end the call. There is no hunter left who is capable of bringing me what I desire."

"Yes, Lord Bishop." Fleur watched the holy man leave, wishing more than anything that he could retreat from the disaster in this chamber. The eyes of death stared back at him as he dragged the imposter to the empty animal cart.

"Shall we bury him?" a guard asked as he angled the cart to push it forward. His tunic, white and new only minutes before, was stained with the blood of the dead imposter.

"Dump him with the rest of these." Fleur waved toward the pile of discarded wolf skins.

"He is no animal, Captain," the guard questioned, sickened by the things he had witnessed that day. The acts of murder and violence were an atrocity to his God, and the leaders he had sworn an oath to were monsters.

"The bishop commands it." Fleur clutched the handle of his sword, threatening the guard.

"Yes, Captain." He pushed the burdened cart out into the courtyard where the eager hunters and trappers waited. The guard could not bear to look at the gasping people as a trail of blood dripped behind him.

"What have they done to Greybeck?" one asked, and the guard paused long enough to tell them.

"He was an imposter." He pushed ahead. "If you do not carry a black wolf, I suggest you make your leave before I haul you out like this."

CHAPTER TWENTY

Isolde stepped around the cart, her fingers touching the tightly-thatched cage. It was the worst of her nightmares to see Rasabel inside, but the task of trapping Rasabel had been less dangerous in the light of day. "Shh," she tried to soothe. "You are safe." She did not see the animal—only the woman she loved. If anyone recognized Isolde, or the blackness of Rasa's fur beneath the fire ash, this trickery would be disastrous.

"She seems calmer now," Bylyn said, keeping her distance but standing close enough to pass Isolde the buckets of pig dung they were smearing around the cart.

"The cage is strong." Intan released his mule into the trees, knowing the animal would be found by villagers if their plan failed.

Onyx pushed against the trace and back-strap of the cart harness, jerking the cart into Bylyn. It was obvious the animal was displeased with both her connection to Intan's wobbly wagon and with Rasabel being trapped inside a cage.

"It's alright," Isolde whispered as she stroked the mare's neck. She hoped her tone was more convincing than the way she felt inside. A trap was a trap, no matter who set it. "She's alright, Onyx. We're going to be alright."

Intan paused to appreciate the gentle whispers, hoping more than anything that Isolde was seeing into their future—a future that ended with success.

"I will leave you all," Bylyn said.

Intan touched the girl's shoulder. "Use caution, girl."

"Yes, Father. I will."

Isolde's hug was unexpected. She whispered, "We are counting on you."

The caressing words felt like a cheer, boosting Bylyn's confidence. "I will not fail any of you." She kicked off her boots at the bushes and waded into the river. "Good travels," she said as she disappeared around the bend.

~~~~~~~~~~

Isolde sat beside Intan. The clunky seat of his horse-drawn cart pinched through the fabric of her frock. She looked over her shoulder, keeping an eye on the wolf trapped inside their makeshift cage. The smear of ash clung to the animal's fur, creating a perfect but temporary disguise.

"This plan will work," she whispered.
~~~~~~~~~~

Intan clicked his tongue, hoping Onyx would drive the cart as Rasabel instructed. It was the only way to sneak them into the castle and gain access to the bishop tomorrow.

"Her plan is an excellent one," Intan affirmed. "What is unknown is whether Bylyn can get in the way she came out."

Before night fell, Rasabel explained in detail what they would do. If there was to be a brief moment where the two women could confront the bishop as living, breathing human beings, she knew each of them had to play their part.

Sneaking the caged wolf inside was the first and most important hurdle, as no guard would allow the armed warrior to ride through the gate on a horse as obviously battle-ready as Onyx.

As a fugitive, Bylyn would have to follow her waterway trail in reverse to meet them inside the city. Hiding in the light of day would have its tricky moments, but their ultimate plan was to wait for the sun and moon convergence Intan swore was coming.

"She will find her way in," Isolde said. "I hope her passage is less fragrant than ours. The stench of the straw pile is foul." She fanned her face as they approached the outer bridge leading to the city. A brief visit to the pig farmer had produced the perfect camouflage for hiding the saddle, and the crusted bits on Isolde's garment along with the foul fragrance would prevent the guards from getting too close to her. The piles of manure and straw were a brilliant and convincing part of their plan.

"It's not just the straw." Intan pointed to the smears all over her. "We have to hide you, too."

"I'm no one of consequence." Isolde waved him off. "Not anymore."

"Your eyes and your voice tell a different story," he said.

Isolde cleared her throat, lowered her voice an octave, and spoke from the side of her mouth. "Is this voice better?" It sounded ridiculous.

Intan shook his head. "That is a horrible voice. Perhaps pretend you are mute and your stink will offend them away."

Isolde grunted a tight, short huff. "Are you sure we've covered the gear enough? This doesn't feel right."

"We have covered the horse's saddle and Rasabel's sword with the only thing they would not lower themselves to touch," Intan said. "We have to trust that the manure will prevent a thorough search." He tugged at the cloth she wore as a substitute for Rasa's cloak. "Now cover yourself." He fussed to hide her face. "This won't work if you're recognized."

Isolde wished for the comfort of the plush interior and the scent of her wife that their cloak gave. For the first time in two years she doubted her abilities, and felt unsure if their plan would work. She ducked her head, letting the dirty linens mask her identity as they approached the first guard post.

"Stop," the guard yelled.

Intan pulled on the reins. "Yes, sir."

"Another foul animal?" He leaned in. "It smells like you rolled it in a dung pile."

"We were told there is a bounty on wolves," Intan said. "This one was a beast to catch. We trapped it going after the pigs." He chortled as Onyx tugged the cart, jerking it to a second stop. "Settle down, there."

A second guard turned around, interested in the horse's jumpiness. "Another wolf, you say?" He was tired of the parade of animals, bored with their lack of difference, and if he never saw another wolf again he would celebrate. He fanned to wave the stench from his nose.

"I've never seen such a monstrous wolf," the first guard said, drawing his sword.

"Remember, Captain Fleur is collecting wolves for the Bishop." The second guard pushed the blade away. "He will have your head if this is the one he's looking for." He poked at the animal and it bared bright white fangs. "Ride on and take the animal to the armory stables. There are a dozen more trappers waiting to see the captain."

"So we will." Intan snapped the reins and Onyx rode on.

Isolde remained cautious as the cart heaved forward. "We're in," she whispered.

"Now to find a place to hide until sunrise."

Isolde thought about all the hiding places she'd had as a child in Mondurey. If they were there, she'd know where to go, but this was Acadia and Acadia was never truly her home.

As they rode through the streets, the interior fortifying walls brought emotions she hadn't prepared to experience. The fountain streams ran, spitting arches of water for the townspeople to enjoy. She'd sat with Rasabel on a few occasions, dipping her toes in the pool, enjoying moments of rest together. Isolde's soul ached as she remembered…

"I am not yours to keep, not a possession a treasury can hold. As hours turn to days, years together are precious as gold." Rasa paused to adjust the page. The folded pieces of parchment came from a peddler she'd met on her journey to Mondurey. The words were sappy and rhyming, which she disliked, but Isolde seemed to enjoy every one.

These were romantic moments they seized—intimate afternoons by the fountains without weapons in their hands. So close and yet fearful to touch.

Taking advantage of Rasabel's reading pause, Isolde said, "I will never call this town home." She wanted to thread her hand through the crook of Rasa's arm and lean against her shoulder, but she did not. Rumor of such behavior in the light of day would spread too fast.

"Acadia?" Rasa asked.

"Yes." Isolde nodded. "I think I'd hate this place if it wasn't for—"

"The armory?" Rasa interrupted, a mischievous grin on her face.

"Is that what you think?" Isolde looked up. "That I like my toys so much?"

Rasa set down the parchment. "I think you enjoy every toy I have taught you to use." She yearned to hold Isolde's hand, to *press it to her heart. "And I include myself in that list."*

"Bel," Isolde whispered. They were living and loving on stolen time, knowing the bishop would demand what he believed was his, hiding their love in shadowed places. "I wish I could kiss you right now." Isolde whispered.

"You kiss me and I forget everything," Rasa confessed. "And that would be unsafe."

"My warrior." There was sorrow in Isolde's eyes, "Love should not leave you defenseless."

"Oh, but for you I would lay down my sword. I swear it."

Isolde inched her hand close, never touching Rasabel's. "I would never ask you to."

Rasa leaned down, wishing she could kiss her. "And that is why I would."

Isolde's memories of the town brought fresh wounds to her already-broken heart. Tears glazed her eyes as they passed the armory. This city was haunted—filled with memories of what was, what should have been, and what might never be. She recognized everything that was stolen from them; hopefully, if their plan went well, they would be stealing it back.

No, Acadia would never be her home.

~~~~~~~~~~

"This journey smells worse than it did the last time I made it," Bylyn whispered. With the aid of a stick bundle, she floated atop the river, guided more by scent than moonlight. The water was littered with the remains of fur and animal entrails drifting by on her route. It was almost like following bread crumbs, but not as enticing.

"It's lunacy, I tell you," a man grumbled as he tossed remains into the water, missing Bylyn's camouflaged head by inches.

"Will he kill every creature that looks like a wolf?" another man said as he dumped a bucket of entrails. Their bickering continued, fading into the darkness.

Bylyn worried about the plan; Isolde and Intan were leading the giant wolf to slaughter. "Go faster," she encouraged herself, wishing again that she knew how to hold her breath and move beneath the water. "They must be warned." She reached for a clump of fur and attached it to her floating stick bundle, hiding herself until she reached the tunnels.

She was sure she would remember most of the way through, but if she didn't, the twists and turns from her struggles had gouges and scratches from the desperate moments of that terrifying escape. If she did not adore Rasa and Isolde the way she did, there was no force living or dead that could convince her to traverse this waterway for a second time.

"I could have hidden in that cart," she mumbled as she swam, catching a bit of the liquid in her mouth. "Pft," she spat, making it worse by taking in more. "I make an oath to you, Goddess. If I survive this water's depth, I will
~~~~~~~~~~

live a better life." At that moment, she realized she could touch the bottom of the tunnel floor. "I hear you, Goddess, and if it isn't a bother, could we also make it out alive?" She didn't waste a moment as she shuffled toward the gate she'd opened during her dungeon escape.

"It must be close to sunrise," she mumbled. "I need to hurry."

~~~~~~~~~~

"I admit, the way your body reshapes from animal to human is not a thing I ever want to witness again," Intan said as he poured hot water into the wash basin. When Isolde and Rasa had transformed from creature to human in the earthy pit the morning before, he'd been distracted dressing Bylyn's wounds.

"Becoming flesh has only felt painful to me once before," Rasa said as she wiped the ash from her skin.

Intan looked at her and somehow knew she was speaking of their failed attempt to trap her. Neither he nor Bylyn could have understood the cruelty in that moment. "I am sorry we had to do it the way we did."

Rasa snickered. "Isolde can be very persuasive when she makes up her mind."

"Your little sprite had a hand in it, too." He dropped a cloth on the table so she could dry her body.

"I'm not going to ask how you managed a bath for me in this barn or how you acquired a uniform tunic for me to wear, but it will make travel easier when I go to confront the Bishop." Rasa stepped into her riding trousers.

"There are many here who will stand beside you, and beside Isolde as well." He bundled the dirty linens. "We all
~~~~~~~~~~

know what was done to you. And as you said, Isolde can be very persuasive."

The hawk sat on the perch behind them, oblivious to the decisions being made on her behalf. Rasa removed a cup of leather from her saddle bag. "I will cover her eyes for you, Intan, so she will not take flight," Rasa explained. She hushed the bird. "You must keep calm, my love," Rasa whispered as if speaking to her wife in human form. She twirled the talon bindings around the makeshift perch, tethering the hawk in place.

Rasa turned to address Intan. "You must promise me that if those church bells ring, you will not make her suffer without me." She clasped the belt around her waist. "If they ring, our plan has failed."

"I cannot take her life." Intan's voice broke. He knew this request would come. As much as the man trusted his own visions, he also knew failure was possible. If what he saw in his visions was not true, Rasa was headed toward a terrible and certain death.

"I cannot damn her to a half life. It is cruel to leave her to face nights without me, and days of this." She pointed at her hawk, at the animal's inability to discern a state of human existence from the pedestal beneath her. "I beg you, do not let her live this way, Intan."

"I will do it." Tears fell from his eyes. "I swear I will."

"I have to trust you will." Rasa pulled the leather gloves over her hands. "All we need now is for our little sprite to open the great hall doors and let me in."

"Will you wait a little longer?" Intan stared out the open window, willing the progress of the sun to shade and the moon to shine so the curse would end. "I swear there will be a chance for the two of you to confront the bishop together."

"It has been two years." Rasa cinched the horse's saddle tighter and left the load of saddlebags and traveling gear with the priest.

"What is one more day?" he begged. "A few more hours?"

"Father, whatever is coming will come," Rasa said as she dropped the stirrup into place. Onyx was ready. "My sword." She held a hand to him, expecting the blade to appear.

Intan resisted. "If I don't give it to you?"

"Old man, there is nothing that will keep me from killing the bishop today." Rasa guided her horse closer to him. "Nothing!"

Intan waddled to the cart, the empty cage a reminder of the night before and the minimal hours of rest he'd had in the last few days. The blade was in its sheath, wrapped in delicate lavender linen. "She said she believes in you and puts her faith in your sword."

Rasa did not speak as she untangled the fabric from her weapon. It smelled of saddlebag leather but It belonged to Isolde. She wrapped the linen around her neck and tucked the ends against the bare skin of her chest. Today it would end, with or without revenge, and she was prepared to not survive.

CHAPTER TWENTY-ONE

Bylyn climbed from the tunnel, drenched in the scent of sewage and wet to the bone. She could not retrace her original path as the horrible drop she had experienced during her escape was impossible to navigate. She found an opening in the street beneath the market, putting her very close to the great hall and her final destination.

Bylyn knew she could not travel through the city of Acadia smelling like a sewer rat. Pretending to be drunk, she slumped her shoulders and stumbled through the crowded market. The reaction of the patrons was as she expected. She was noticed, but only enough for people to get away from the sight and smell.

"Ex-cuse me, sir," she slurred. "Could ya spare a piece of bread for me?" she asked the baker at his stand.

He pushed her toward the street. "You reek, girl. Get away before you scare my paying customers."

"S-sorry s-ir." She stumbled drunk again. Most people avoided her from the stench alone but she got close enough to pick the pocket of a trader balancing a heavy load of animal furs on his shoulder.

She hid behind a cart of rotten fruit to check the contents of the drawstring pouch she'd stolen. More than thirty copper coins, she guessed. The theft would set her up for weeks if she left the city now, but the thought was fleeting as she remembered the sacrifices Intan, Isolde and Rasabel were making.

She looped the coin pouch through her corded belt, excited she wouldn't have to wash in an animal trough. Able to pay for a proper session, she entered a bath house far from the town center.

"A clean water wash, please?" she asked the woman hanging wet linens.

The woman turned, covering her face to block the smell. "You'll be needing more than a bath." She fanned her face.

Bylyn thought of the time. Lowering her voice, she said, "Just hot water, please." She followed the woman through the bathhouse and out the door. The open shed held a metal basin filled with water less than shin deep.

"Can't have you washin' that off inside," the woman said, realizing the foul-scented man was in fact a young woman. "I'll pull the curtain to give ya privacy." She tugged the linen fabric around Bylyn.

Moments later, the attendant returned to set a container of steaming water on the table beside the tub.

Bylyn had dreamed of luxurious hot baths but she would barely have time to enjoy this scalding rinse.

"Two coppers." The attendant held out her hand.

Bylyn felt the pouch tied to her waist. The amount seemed high but she didn't have time to haggle.

The attendant waited as Bylyn stripped before making the first pour for her to wash. "You'll need fresh things to wear, dear," she said, eager to take Bylyn's foul clothes.

"I have two more copper coins." Bylyn knew she had ten times that amount but she didn't want choices.

The woman returned with a smock, a pair of sandals and a hooded linen robe. "If this suits you?" she asked.

"That will do perfectly." Left alone, the girl plunged the rag and scrubbed her skin. The pool at her feet was the color of mud, and she knew she was hardly clean as she wiped the water from her body and slipped on the fresh clothes.

"To cover your head." The attendant held a linen scarf. "It is horrible what they do to you in there."

She knows, Bylyn thought.

"I will not tell." The woman unfolded the material, draping it over Bylyn's shoulders before wrapping it securely to mask her face.

"Thank you," Bylyn said as she exited the bath house. The scarf felt comforting against her face even if a little scratchy. It was nothing like the plush cloak that Rasa wore, but comfort was not important to their plan.

Much like the people bustling toward the bishop's festivities, Bylyn appeared inconsequential as she threaded herself through the crowd.

"Are ya headed to see the bishop?" a man asked.

Bylyn nodded, slowing so he would move on, and then followed him to the great hall. She rushed past the guards standing watch, tipping her face away so they could not see her. She dropped a copper coin in the fountain as she passed, making a single wish: "Let Intan's vision come true." A few minutes later, she passed through the massive archway, pausing briefly to admire the locking mechanism on the door. She'd done it. She'd made it inside.

Her part of the plan had officially begun.

~~~~~~~~~~

"Dare I ask how you came to have these uniform pieces?" Rasabel asked as she folded her cloak.

"We decided hiding in plain sight was the best way to get you past the great hall battalion," Intan explained, using excessive vigor as he wiped down the wash basin to avoid making eye contact.

"Who is this we?" Rasa grinned, guessing the answer and also delighting that Isolde was still tactical in her thinking.

"Your wife and I," he said. With Isolde's talent for distraction, they had managed to relieve a youthful guard of his tunic and helmet.

"I approve." Rasa slipped the tunic over her head. "And this?" She put on the helmet before fastening the strap beneath her chin.

"That was Isolde, too. She said you would approve." Intan adjusted the feathered plume on the right side of the headpiece, celebrating internally that he'd finally done
~~~~~~~~~~

something right. "We thought a uniformed guard would be free to go anywhere today."

"You thought correctly." Rasa was pleased with the garb, agreeing it would be impossible for a commoner to enter the guarded area on foot, carrying a sword, and bow openly. "Then the plan is set, as long as our little sprite gets me in."

Rasa kicked into a stirrup, adjusted herself in the saddle and spurred Onyx forward. With her face covered by the stolen helmet, she moved easily through the city dressed as a guard. She kept her sword handle covered, passing a dozen trained watchmen before approaching the crucial test of her disguise.

"Take a position near the open gate," Captain Fleur ordered as Rasa stopped beside three mounted patrol members. She followed the command, her heart racing with the knowledge that the Bishop was less than thirty yards away. She'd dreamt of this day for two long years. Her hands ached as she steadied herself against the urge for revenge.

The horse raised her head once, indicating her awareness that a fight was forthcoming. Rasa and Onyx stayed in sync, grateful that their years of training hadn't faded with time. They knew how to move, how to ride as if they were meant to be present beside these soldiers, because not so long ago they were.

"Close the doors," the captain yelled to the guards as he walked through the archway.

Rasa waited, positioning herself in front of the oversized stone and metal partition as the only way inside slammed shut. Patience was the action of the moment as the lock clicked tight. "It is your turn now, Little Sprite," she said as she waited, listening for the festivities to begin on the other side.

~~~~~~~~~~

Bylyn stayed close to the wall, her gauzy clothes clinging to the jagged stonework as she crept through the crowd inside the massive space. She had never been invited to such a festival, and paused to appreciate the ornamentation on the attendants' garments. Her ragged second-hand clothing stood out amongst the gowns trimmed with lace and fresh flowers, separating the working class from the wealthy. It was so much like a Christening for babies, but these were all grown women hoping to find favor with a lustful and pious man.

Bylyn carried Rasabel's small dagger against her forearm, the handle sweaty in her palm. She'd picked an uncountable number of locks in her lifetime. This one would not be different, but the result would be freedom better than any treasure.

She could not fail.

In a grand fashion, the bishop entered. The Captain of the Guard stood near the staged altar, positioning himself so the holy man was the center of attention. Their linens were the brightest white Bylyn had ever seen, hurting her eyes to almost blindness.

She sidestepped the crowd at the back of the hall until she reached the door. She'd had time to contemplate the locking mechanism. It was not complex but it would take time. She shoved the blade inside, tilting it left, then right. The first click was the loudest, and she turned to see if it drew attention from any of the guests. The music
~~~~~~~~~~

played on and she continued, knowing there were two more levers to release. The noon hour bells of the cathedral rang, signaling she was right on time.

Captain Fleur clapped and chanted to the music, watching the crowd for mischief, glancing at every entrance. Bylyn's modest appearance caught his eye and he made his way toward her. He adjusted the handle of his sword, prepared to take down the intruder, knowing the person in that garment did not belong.

"What are you doing there?" he asked, his voice low and drowned by the song and dance.

She ignored his question. Her tongue jutted, as she forced the dagger toward the final release of the lock.

"I asked what you are doing there," he repeated.

Bylyn felt the ting of the lever catching. "I am unlocking this door." She chuckled as the final click released the mechanism.

Before the captain could react, the massive timber door swung open, banging against the wall with the full force of a rider to move it.

Bylyn stumbled away, hoping to hide from the captain as he took in the magnificence of the horse and the tunic-draped rider on top.

Rasa charged in, Onyx stepping with confidence, the clomp of hooves echoing as they met the marble floors. "Hello again, Captain Fleur." Rasa clutched her sword handle, anticipating what was to come. The helmet hid her face but not her voice.

"Rasabel!" the captain yelled as he stumbled out of their path. He pulled the stunned perimeter guard from his horse and kicked into the saddle. He felt his burn wounds from his confrontation with Rasabel, and the blisters tore where they snagged his uniform fabric. It would be a challenge to face the former captain this way.

Rasa did not stop as she searched the room, her eyes focusing on a single target. The Bishop was impossible to miss in his long white robes. The holy man clung to his women as the festivities stopped for the rider's approach.

Row by row, the crowd fell silent as Onyx trotted forward. This horse and its rider were not official guards of Acadia.

Bylyn watched, waiting for her next role in the plan. Intan snuck around the doorway, passing the weapon to the girl. "Good luck." He disappeared, returning to care for the tethered hawk.

"Don't be limp like a worm." Bylyn whispered Rasa's first rule to herself. "Release, don't let go." She slipped the bracer over her forearm and gripped the strings with her teeth to draw it tight. "You can do this. Bow to cheek, keep a line." She heard Rasa's voice in her head as she repeated the three rules over and over. "You can do this. They need you to do this." It was impossible to believe that she, a little thief and liar, could be more than those few words.

"Rasabel!" the captain screamed again as he charged toward her. "You don't belong here."

Onyx dipped her head, pivoting around as Rasa drew her sword hidden beneath the tunic, seconds before the Captain of the Guard slammed his weapon at her shoulder.

"You dare to enter the House of the Lord bearing arms." The captain swung his blade, using the power of jealousy and hate to take her down, but his horse was not trained for face-to-face sword fighting.

Rasa's smile was all he could see beneath the helmet as she countered his predictable moves. Her blade slashed through the bracer on his forearm and he screamed. The battle seemed one-sided.

As if Onyx understood the next maneuver, she moved in perfect step with Rasa's fighting style. It was evident the new Captain of the Guard was no match for the old one.

Their swords clashed, edges clanging against the other, as the crowd moved from the center of the hall, giving way for the two horses and their fighters.

Commanding the advantage, Rasa slipped a foot from the stirrup and kicked high at Fleur's hip, knocking him from his saddle. Without a second glance, she rode forward, each echoing clomp of Onyx's hooves drawing her closer to the bishop.

Rasa wondered why the warning bells did not ring. She looked across the hall at the hanging pull rope. The bell ringer dangled, lifeless, pinned to the door by a single arrow through the heart.

Bylyn stood holding a bow with her final arrow nocked against it. She could hold off one more bell ringer.

Rasa had no time to waste. She tapped her heels against Onyx's sides, the same time Captain Fleur ripped at the reins. The leather strands slipped through Rasabel's hand and the horse jerked back, tossing Rasabel from the saddle. Agility and muscle memory made it easy for her to land on her feet as the horse shuffled sideways, trying her best to protect the tumbling rider.

Rasa patted the animal. "Go." Onyx back-stepped but did not run. She was as much a part of the fight as Rasabel.

"You won't have it so easy." Fleur spat as he raised his blade again.

Rasa unclasped her helmet, dropping it to the floor. "Let's end this now," she growled. Her fight was not with this man, but he was the last obstacle in her path to the Bishop. She deflected the blade strike, spinning backward to elbow him in the gut. Good fortune followed her today as she realized the man wore no armor or chainmail beneath his uniform.

"You've been away too long, Rasabel," he taunted, thinking she'd be easy to kill, surrounded by dozens of men at his command.

"I have lived for revenge, Fleur. It has kept me satisfied with an empty belly, and warm on cold days." Their blades clashed and she stepped close enough to feel his breath on her face.

"I would think it was the cursed fur covering your filthy skin keeping you warm and alone." He attempted to strike her forehead with his own, but she spun free.

His words did not hurt the way he thought and she did not ease up or collapse with weakness. She'd lived every day as if it was her last, never knowing what would hunt her in the dark of night. She thought of Isolde as she deflected the next blade swing. No, there was little she feared any longer. She rounded once, striking Fleur in the temple with an elbow.

The crowd of onlookers did not interfere, stunned silent as their captain stumbled to the floor. His head struck the surface and he lay unconscious.

Rasa tapped his cheek with the tip of her blade. "All words with no skill behind them." She pushed his torso with her boot. Content that the man would not rise, she set her sights on the bishop.

The holy man's satisfied smirk vanished as he realized his captain was not recovering. He mumbled words Rasa could not hear, a blessing or perhaps another curse, but whatever it was struck fear in the eyes of the closest guests and they moved away.

Rasa felt dizzy, lightheaded and unsure on her feet. Her hands trembled, shaking as if the room had suddenly become cold. Her blade clattered as it fell to the polished marble floor. The pain in her back was real as she collapsed to her knees. "No," she whispered. "I cannot fail now."

CHAPTER TWENTY-TWO

Rasabel clutched her chest, feeling a sensation she could not define. There was no blood as she patted her body, no outside wound that she could find, yet it felt like her soul was ripping from her flesh.

Darkness fell over the room and she thought surely death had found her this day.

"The sky!" a woman yelled, pointing to the sun. The crowd watched in stunned silence as the bluest of skies, cloudless and almost blinding in its hue, began to hide in the forthcoming shadow.

The warrior could not believe the darkness. Was this sensation in her body not a wound but the end of the bishop's curse? "A day without a night," Rasa whispered to herself as she felt the sting of a fist against her side. She fell, stunned and desperate. The bishop's curse unraveling inside her was disorienting, slowing her reaction as she turned to confront her attacker.

"Fleur, you'll not win this fight." Rasa scowled as her punch landed against his cheek. "I am not like the guards or women you're accustomed to beating." She grabbed the robe he wore, twisting it at his throat. "You are not part of my fight. Yield, or you will perish this day."

He punched his dagger at Rasa's ribs and she deflected with the bracer on her forearm. If not for the leather band, the strike would have been a killing blow. Rasa felt no sting of a wound, and Fleur's eyes grew wide with horror as Rasa pushed him to the floor.

He surrendered to her grasp, expecting that it would be his final breath.

"Rasa!" Bylyn screamed as she launched her last arrow, striking the bellringer's shoulder.

The next few seconds passed like hours as Rasa watched the wounded guard fall against the rope, the heaviness of his body setting the counterweight in motion. As long as the man was tangled to this tether, the bell would ring.

There was no time to stop the sound.

The bells sounded once and twice and over again.

"No!" Rasabel screamed.

It was a sound Bylyn would never forget as she watched the warrior fall to her knees in absolute surrender. This could not be true. Intan would have no way to know the battle wasn't over. If he honored Rasa's request, Isolde was already dead. Bylyn stumbled, the bow falling from her hand, but the sound of the wooden weapon hitting the marble floor was lost in the bell's heartless chimes.

Rasa could not clear her vision as the world disappeared, but her muscles remembered what to do even if her soul fell numb. This was what she'd spent her days training for, what she lived and breathed these last two years.

Fueled by rage and blind with unbearable grief, Rasa's fist met Fleur's cheek as he stood, dropping the man back to the floor. She did not care about anything but revenge, blind with grief knowing each strike was energy wasted on her path to the man cowering on the altar. The bishop was her real fight now. With Fleur's dagger in one hand and her sword in the other, Rasa charged toward her target.

The alarm bells stopped and the warrior's heart felt empty. Revenge was all that was left.

Fleur staggered to his feet. "Are you running from the fight, Captain Rasabel?" His snigger was sinister, taunting in a way that violated Rasa's belief in honor.

She pivoted to face him. "You are as dumb as you are unskilled." She did not hold back and her sword came down with the full force of her body.

He had no time to react—no gasp, no expression. There was only a single whole-body movement striking him a final time, severing his head from the rest of his body. Rasa stared, taking in the victory without celebration before turning toward the bishop. There was no one left to stand between them. The curse would end today and she didn't care what remained of her when it was over.

She steadied her blood-covered blade, her vision tunneling with a single purpose as she advanced toward the bishop.

"Guards!" the holy man commanded, but no one moved. They knew who Rasabel was and what she'd survived even before striking Fleur down, and they would not defend whatever wickedness the bishop commanded. It was possible she could save them all.

Rasa stood a stone's throw from pure evil. "There is no one left to protect you," she said with more control than she felt. Her feet were weightless as she stepped closer.

"If you kill me, Captain, you damn yourself forever."

"Forever," she repeated as if it wasn't a killing blow. "It means nothing to me now."

The bishop's grin was vicious as he targeted her one and only weakness. "Is revenge more important than Isolde?"

Rasa rotated her blade and pointed it at the man, the weight of it feeling impossible to hold. She wanted to drop it down across his throat, cutting this evil leader in two. Killing him was what she'd desired for two years, and the finality of it was a punch to her gut. She wanted him to feel two years of torture in a single breath. "Isolde—is—dead!" she screamed, jerking the sword above her head to strike. "And your death will bring me great joy—"

"Bel." The sound of her voice halted everything in the room.

Rasa did not believe what she was hearing as stopping the killing swing nearly knocked her to her knees. *It is sorcery*, Rasa thought—some evil work of the bishop she could not trust. She did not dare turn around, knowing a knife would surely find her back. She watched the bishop's narrowed eyes of vengeance widen with disbelief.

"Bel?"

It was more of a question now, but no other living soul would call her by such an intimate name. She was an angel; her angel. Rasa wanted to cover her ears to block the sound, but what if when she turned around Intan's prophecy became the truth? Only her Isolde could call her in a way that made the heart tremble. All those nights she dreamed of hearing it; could it be Isolde in the flesh? The sword dipped, the heavy steel weighted from two years of solitary longing, replacing it with hope that she thought was impossible after all this time. Trusting her body to know when Isolde was near, she turned around. "It… how can this be?" Rasa could not look away.

The moment felt otherworldly as Intan stumbled in with a dagger clutched tight for defense.

"My wife," Rasa whispered, not believing what her eyes could see. *Intan's vision,* she thought. *The collision of day and night is real.*

The chasm between woman and beast was closed as Isolde walked between rows and rows of astonished onlookers.

Rasa stumbled over her sword as she approached her beloved wife, defenseless against this one who owned her soul. "Isolde," Rasa's tone was hushed as she reached out to touch her, yearning for every sense to confirm that the physical body standing before her was real.

Isolde trembled, remembering her lover with that single caress. There was no time for the reunion she wanted as the room fell deeper into darkness. "This is not a dream," Isolde whispered. "We must confront him now."

Rasa nodded, knowing their day with night was temporary. Together, they had to address the creator of their curse. Isolde did not let go as Rasa held her hand, drawing the two of them together as they walked toward the bishop.

Rasa picked up her blood-covered blade, ready to take revenge.

Isolde glimpsed the decapitated captain, and without a second glance she walked forward. The marble floor was cold against her bare feet, and the hand holding hers reminded her that her flesh was as real as her wife's.

After two years, the bishop was lost to age and spite. No longer regal, his face had wrinkled and he'd grown weak from gluttony brought on by lust and greed. *He* was the sinfulness he preached would bring damnation. Isolde found no pleasure in these observations.

His nose creased as if the scent of love was foul to smell. "You cannot be." He scowled.

"But we can." Rasa raised her blade to his face. "We are here."

He turned away, getting tangled in his long robe as he tried to escape.

"Stop!" Rasa yelled. "You cannot run from what you've done."

The bishop froze, not from the command but from her audacity to make one. "You dare—" He turned to Rasa, fearful to see the two of them standing side by side. With his full weight resting against the staff, he cowered behind his gloved hand.

Rasa leapt at him. "Look at me, you monster!" she yelled as she pressed the edge of her blade to his throat.

He peeked between his trembling fingers.

"Look!" she yelled again, and the man's hand fell away. "Now look at her." She ripped his arm down away from his face. "Look—at—my—wife!"

He gasped. The title of wife was an impossibility. He had never married them, never signed their union in the eyes of his god. Marriage was the joining of two in the flesh— unachievable in these two years—but the look in Rasabel's eyes said it was true. The bishop could do nothing else as he stared upon Isolde's beautiful face.

She was as heavenly as he remembered; fair skin he wanted to caress, rosy lips he desired on his body, but the eyes—Isolde's soulful eyes could cut a man into pieces. The bishop saw something more, something time did to a girl as she became a woman.

Rasa pushed him and he stumbled against the banquet table. "Now look at us." Rasa spat the words as the man's gaze fell upon them. *Could it be this simple to end two years of suffering?* she wondered. She dropped her sword. The clatter echoed through the great hall as the light of day broke through the dark.

She was still there. Isolde was still there, standing on two feet in human form, as breathtaking as the first day they'd met.

Isolde touched Rasa's shoulder but did not stop as she took her turn with the bishop.

To the self-absorbed man, it appeared as if Isolde wanted him, as she bypassed Rasabel to approach him. A grin of satisfaction grew on his face. She was a woman now, not the girl who'd been in his care; perhaps she understood what power could do. Isolde's arms stretched as if to hug him and he held his hands to welcome her in.

This would be her moment as the bird's blinding cap fell to the floor. One at a time, she threw the tether strands at the bishop's face. "Now this curse belongs to you."

Isolde's disgust was clear and felt like daggers to the bishop's heart. He winced as the pieces slapped his skin. She did not want him. She did not need him. She only wanted freedom from him, and the bindings were his final strangling hold.

Isolde turned away, wanting more than anything to touch her wife. Rasa stood as she had always been, unarmed in her heart and defenseless in her soul against the woman who was the love of her life.

The bishop could not bear the sight of these women rejecting his power, rejecting him. He anchored his staff against his gaudy chair, plucking the protective cover from the hidden spear. "You will never find happiness." He lunged forward to stab Isolde in the back. "If you are not mine, then you are no one's." The distance between them was wide as he rotated the staff to pierce her spine. Isolde was steps ahead of him, her hand raised an arm's length away from caressing her wife's adoring face.

"Rasa!" Intan and Bylyn yelled at the same moment.

There was no hesitation as the warrior moved, rolling across the marble floor instinctively, her hands reaching for the sword, but she was too slow. There would be no regret from her for seeking revenge this day or ever; Isolde would carry that weight.

Isolde dropped to her knee, her hand steady, confident in her actions as she grasped the blade at her feet. The spin was smooth, the memory of practiced muscles exercised to fight, trained to survive in the dark of night. Without hesitation, or drift, the sword flew with deadly accuracy as it speared through the bishop's heartless chest.

The room echoed with a collective gasp.

Isolde's body heaved as she fought the emotions hammering through her body. She stepped forward, needing to stare into his eyes, knowing he was aware that as his life drained away, hers was born anew.

This would not be undone. There was no one left to chase her from the life she desired. She stood, statue still, as his eyes lost the last light of life.

"Isolde." Rasa touched her wife's shoulder.

Isolde could not turn around, fearful this was a fever dream from her arrow wound and she would wake alone. She closed her eyes, her head falling back against a warm body, wishing it to be true.

Rasa knew how to break the spell of disbelief as she leaned close, whispering, "Is."

Isolde's hand trembled as she covered her mouth. She turned around. Rasa stood in human form, and Isolde's lonely dreams—those she begged for in the dark of night—became her truth.

Rasa ripped off her gloves and held out her hand. "Touch me. Believe I am real."

"Can this be true?" Isolde wept.

"It is the truest truth," Rasa whispered as her lips touched the back of her wife's hand.

Isolde gasped. "Bel," she sobbed. "My Bel." She fell into Rasa's embrace. Strong arms came around her, lifting her from the ground.

"Isolde." Rasa buried her face against Isolde's chest, breathing in new life. She set her down, and her hand trembled as her fingertips traced the lines of Isolde's tears. "You must pinch me. I cannot tell if I'm awake or if I'm dreaming."

Isolde tipped up onto her toes, her lips feather light against her wife's. A breath apart, she whispered, "It is as real as my love for you." She kissed her again.

"Is," Rasa whispered.

"My Bel." Isolde smiled, feeling the solid brawn of her wife's body for the first time in two years.

"Captain Rasabel." A guard cleared her throat, not eager to interrupt the strange reunion but unclear what to do about the bloodbath in the great hall.

Rasa turned, keeping her wife tight to her side. "I am not your Captain," she argued.

"Since you are the last one standing, I would proclaim that you are." She stood at attention, calling to every uniformed person in the great hall to do the same. "We are at your command, Captain."

Rasa stripped away the uniform tunic and all the constraints it implied. She could never return to the life she'd lived before the curse, but this wasn't the time to argue positions of power. "What is your name?"

"Anayn, Captain."

Rasa shook her head. "It is now the reverse." She placed her hand on the guard's shoulder. "You have taken the vow to guard Acadia?" she asked.

"I have," Anayn said.

"As Captain of the Guard, I relinquish my duties and hereby pass them to you." Rasa smiled. "Captain Anayn."

"But Capt—"

Rasa raised a wiggling finger in disapproval. "Not anymore. Now go take charge of the former leader and what is left of him."

"Yes—" Anayn caught herself before calling her Captain. "You heard Rasabel," she yelled and the guards began the task of cleaning up the great hall.

The crowd moved; some came to gawk and inspect the gruesome scene while others fled, fueled by superstition and worry about what wrath might come.

Rasa noticed Intan and Bylyn headed toward the archway exit. "Wait," she yelled and two guards sidestepped, blocking anyone from leaving. "Bring them to me."

Isolde turned, grounding herself with her back tight against Rasa's chest.

Bylyn did not like the guard's arm holding her bicep or the push forcing her into the center of the great hall. Intan went willingly, ready to celebrate the end of the curse and whatever punishment might follow for his part in it.

"Captain." The escort pushed them forward and Rasa snickered at the use of the title. It would take a few hours for them to learn of Anayn's new position.

Isolde did not wait for an invitation and reached for the man, embracing him with a hug. "Thank you," she said. "You didn't give up on us."

Intan knew that was untrue. His betrayal of a sacred moment had set the terrible curse in motion, but forgiveness was all he could ever need. "It is over." He wiped his tears.

"It is over," Rasa agreed but did not follow with a hug. She would need more time for forgiveness.

Bylyn twisted the flapping end of the belt around her waist, nervously witnessing the exchange. Love was an emotion she had not known, but the sight of Isolde and Rasa together left a wonder-filled feeling inside her.

Isolde was more beautiful in the light of day, and her gray eyes no longer carried the dullness of sorrow.

"My little sprite." Rasa's hand cupped the back of her neck, drawing the girl closer. "You are the blessing I did not know I would find when I chased after those damn warning bells."

"An unbelievable friend," Isolde whispered.

Bylyn stared at the floor, the light of their joy so blinding she could not bear to see it. "No one has ever called me a blessing nor a friend." She chuckled. "Criminal, mostly. Liar, probably and always, always a thief."

"You are those no more." Rasa tipped the girl's chin so they were eye-to-eye. "You are those no more. Do you hear me?"

Isolde leaned close, placing a feather-light kiss on the girl's cheek. "You are..." She held her tears. "You have... I cannot find the right words of gratitude, but we are so blessed that we found you."

Bylyn felt weightless as Isolde's affection sparked new confidence in her. She could be different. She could be more than a thief if she let these feelings live inside her. She stumbled away, steading herself against Intan's wobbly walk.

"I cannot believe, Father," she mumbled, "but it is impossible not to when they stand together."

"They have that effect on you, don't they?" he said.

"More than I ever thought any two people could."

"What will you do now, Bylyn?" he asked as they stepped into the afternoon light—a wobbly old man and a girl in her tattered frock blending into the crowd.

She giggled. "I know a ruined building that could use some fixing." She elbowed him in the side.

"Do you, now?" He rubbed the spot pretending it hurt more than it did.

She nodded. "And if that mule of a horse can carry two, perhaps you'll take me there?"

"I can do that," he agreed.

"That's enough," she said. "I think that's enough for now."

Chapter Twenty-Three

The lovers felt the eyes of Acadia upon them as they moved toward the bishop's body. Rasa planted her boot against the dead man's chest before ripping her sword from his heart. His blood pooled at her feet, but she did not celebrate as she thought she would. He was a man, like any other, but his desire to possess what he did not deserve was his undoing. There were no sorrowful cries for the loss of this soul. What a terrible legacy.

His curse destroyed too many things, she thought as his blood clouded her view. The silence of the crowd behind her was terribly loud. There were no guards to fight and no demands of retribution for the bishop's death. Rasa looked at the guests, stunned silent by what she and Isolde had done. By freeing themselves from the bishop's powers, they'd also set everyone in the territory free.

This moment did not seem possible after so much time. Rasa clenched the killing sword in her left hand and felt the gentle squeeze of Isolde's fingers in her right. She was no longer alone, no longer adrift in an ocean of solitude. "Isolde," she whispered.

"Yes." Isolde waited. It had been two years and yet the seconds they stood together beside the bishop's body felt like a lifetime.

For the first time since the curse was cast, Rasa was afraid. "It feels like I'm dreaming," she said. "If I look up, will it be you I see?"

Isolde smiled. "You are not dreaming." She touched Rasa's chin, tipping her face. "We are here, together."

"Is," Rasa whispered.

"Yes." Tears fell from Isolde's eyes and Rasa wiped them away. They stood together for a long moment, afraid to move and break this sacred spell.

"Where do we go now?" Isolde asked, uncertain what awaited her in the light of day. She was accustomed to the quiet, peopleless silence of night.

"Anywhere you'd like, my love." Rasa pulled her wife closer, tucking the smaller woman in the shelter of her arm. "First, we will find my horse." She clicked her tongue and the animal was beside them. "Now, we will leave this place."

"I think I'd like that very much," Isolde whispered through tears. "I don't want to be in Acadia." The great hall felt haunted by memories she was not ready to address. There was no magic blend of herbs to soothe the wounds to her heart.

Rasa stopped, turning Isolde to look at her. "What is it?"

"It is too much in the light of day." Isole trembled as tears fell freely.

"Is." Rasa held her close. "We will not stay."

"Everyone is watching like we are performing for them." Isolde buried herself against Rasa's shoulder.

"We will not stay," Rasa whispered. "My love."

Isolde trembled with tears. "My Bel." Her cheek rubbed against Rasa's bodice armor.

Their mouths were a breath apart as Rasa hesitated. "I fear I no longer know how to kiss you," Rasa admitted.

The kiss was gentle, as tentative as their very first.

Isolde smiled. "My lips say you do." Her fingers traveled into the tangle of long hair. "Overcome that fear, Rasabel, and kiss me again."

Onyx was patient behind them as they stopped many times on their way to the stables, pausing for kisses to remember and for touches that seemed necessary to affirm their reality.

Intan and Bylyn were fastening the cart to a mule from the stable when they noticed the approaching lovers. "They need an inn," Bylyn whispered, delighting in the affection Isolde and Rasa shared.

"Aye, I think you are right."

Bylyn tied the drawstring pouch to the horn of Onyx's saddle. "There are more than twenty coppers in there."

"A great gift that I will not ask how you acquired." Intan frowned with disapproval.

"If you do not ask, we will never speak of it again." Bylyn covered her mouth.

Isolde took the saddle bag from Intan's hand, rummaging through until she found what she wanted. "I have something for you." Rasa held the saddle bag so Isolde could present her gift.

"A gift… for me?" Emotions stifled Bylyn's words. In her eighteen years, she'd never received anything rightfully.

Isolde held the pouch to the girl. "It is for you to practice."

Bylyn slipped the drawstring pouch open, revealing Isolde's precious sling. "M'lady, I cannot."

Isolde covered Bylyn's hand, closing the weapon inside. "You must. I own nothing but what we have carried for two years. This"—she squeezed their hands around the sling— "this is a treasure from my past as much as you are a treasure to me now. You must take it and learn to protect yourself, and when we are together again you will show me what you've learned."

"I swear I will—"

"Please do not swear." Isolde smiled.

Rasa chuckled as she settled the saddlebag across Onyx's shoulders. "Are you returning with Intan?" she asked, noticing the coin pouch immediately. She squeezed it, acknowledging what was inside.

"I am," Bylyn answered. "There is much to be done to make his ruins less ruined."

"Keep it up, girl," Intan grumbled, "and you'll be sleeping in that leaky stable all alone."

Bylyn hopped on the seat of the cart. "You say that like it is a bad thing. You can't imagine some of the places I've slept, or tried to. They'd make your knees ache worse than all that penitent positioning."

"It will be a long ride home if those are the stories you plan to share." He chuckled but it sounded more like a groan.

She held out a hand to help him climb in beside her. "I have many stories that won't cause damnation. I promise you, Father."

Intan adjusted his backside in his seat, watching as Rasa loaded her saddlebag onto the horse. "Where will the two of you go?" he asked.

"It doesn't matter, Father," Isolde said.

Rasa kissed her wife's hand. "Wherever we go, we'll be together and that's all we need for now."

<center>~~~~~~~~~~</center>

Rasabel and Isolde walked through Acadia holding tight to each other with Onyx loaded for the trail ahead. They stopped near the doorway of the armory shed.

"This is the only place I'll miss," Rasa confessed. "The only place I could have visited in these two years."

"You will miss your precious weapons room," Isolde teased.

Rasa swooped her wife into her arms, spinning her around until they pushed through the door. "This room and the one like it in Mondurey. Not the weapons or the garb, but what they were for us. For the history of you and me." She stepped from Isolde's side, positioning the smaller woman's hands out in front of her. Rasa picked up a sword. "These"—she laid one across Isolde's arms—"the weapons used to destroy. " She removed all eight, giving the weight to Isolde.

"They are a little heavy, my love."

Rasa scooped them from her wife's arms and dropped them on the table. "Yes, heavy, but they have been protecting something very important." She pushed the storage rack away from the wall.

"And what would that be?" Isolde knelt beside her wife, curious as she watched her wiggle a stone free from the corner.

Rasa's fingers dipped inside, searching for what could never be replaced. "These." She unwrapped a bundle of cloth, revealing two silver bands.

"Our rings." Isolde choked, fighting the tears glistening her eyes. "That first night"—she closed her eyes, holding tight to the treasure—"I thought... I felt for it on my finger. Everything was confusing, you were gone and my hand was not my own without it. The loss of that ring was one more thing that I thought was gone forever."

"Forever," Rasa repeated, finding the word had less meaning now. She returned each sword to the position she'd found it. "I was lost," she said, "the moment you disappeared and all that remained was a bird chasing the spinning circle that represented my vow to you."

"It was..." Isolde held the rings in her hand. "It was cruel. I didn't know I would leave you with only this." She wiped the tears with the back of her hand.

"Our rings gave me hope that first day," Rasa whispered, tipping Isolde's chin. "Look at me, love." Her thumb caressed Isolde's cheek. "Those rings... our rings reminded me I had to care for you no matter what. In an odd way, they were a guide, showing me that Acadia was no longer a safe place for us."

"So you hid them here?" Isolde didn't understand. "In Acadia?"

"I knew—" Rasa's voice broke. "I knew no one would find them. If I never returned, our rings would stay safe inside these walls."

"Where we became lovers." Isolde forced a smile. "Where I told you I loved you for the very first time."

"Yes," Rasa whispered. "Say it again."

Isolde leaned close. "I love you," she whispered.

Rasabel felt the three words to the tips of her toes. Isolde's voice was the caress she desired in the loneliness of the last two years. Yes, she wanted her body, the heat of passion two lovers shared, but words of love whispered with intimacy were more erotic than she ever believed they could be.

Isolde was pleased, watching Rasabel react the same as she remembered. She knew they were different, twisted and scarred by the curse, but the love was there, stronger than she ever dreamed. She played with the rings in her hand, sizing one as her own and trading it with the other.

"Do you remember what we said in front of our goddess?"

Rasa nodded, opening Isolde's hand. "I remember every word. And you?"

Isolde's smile was forced, tears dripping from her chin. "Like no time has passed." She sobbed.

"Tell me."

Isolde touched the ring to the tip of Rasa's finger. "My heart. My vow."

Rasa closed her eyes, disbelief crushing against this possible reality.

Isolde touched her lips to her wife's, never letting go of her hand. "Open your eyes, Bel."

Rasa was powerless against the command.

Isolde began again, their eyes locked on one another. "My heart. My vow. One love between two that none will divide. My life, bound to yours as long as I am alive." Isolde pushed the ring but it would not pass her second knuckle. "Oh."

Rasa twisted the silver band, forcing it on her finger. "No fear. It is back where it belongs."

"But it will not come off?" Isolde said.

Rasa held Isolde's hand. "As it should have been from the beginning."

"Bel," Isolde whispered.

"Isolde. My heart." Rasabel smiled. "My vow. One love between two that none will divide. My life, bound to yours as long as I am alive." She added her own amendment. "You are my one, and from this day no person and no curse will divide us again." She slid the ring on Isolde's finger. "I think you should kiss me now," she said.

Isolde grinned. "Is that all?"

Rasa took her wife in her arms. "We have not touched for two years, and I fear if we wait another day I might not survive, but this armory is not—"

"Acadia is not the place for us any longer," Isolde interrupted. "I would make love to you against every surface in this armory if I knew we had the protections your position once provided."

Rasa grinned. "Every surface?"

Isolde chuckled. "And every wall in every way I have dreamed for two years." She pressed their palms, fingers tightening as they clasped together.

Rasa swallowed hard. "We could."

"Not here." Isolde turned in her arms, back to front. "We cannot stay in Acadia any longer."

"You are right." Rasa sighed. "But Acadia owes us." She twirled Isolde around and raised her to sit on the tabletop. "What would my lovely wife desire?" She fanned her hands in front of the display of weapons.

"Are you an option?" Isolde winked.

"Yes, I am but later, remember." Rasa grabbed a dozen arrows. "These will replace what Bylyn lost."

"Lost?" Isolde questioned.

"I guess the guards"—Rasa paused to phrase her thought—"received them, so technically they were confiscated."

"Confiscated." Isolde shook her head. "By the guards who are now dead or disfigured?"

"Consequences." Rasa shrugged as she placed a dagger in Isolde's hand. "For your hip."

"We will no longer have to share."

"No, love," Rasa corrected, "we will share it all. Together forever."

<p style="text-align:center">~~~~~~~~~~</p>

The full moon lit the night sky. Rasa lay atop the worn cloak, thumbing the band of silver around her finger. Her skin was warm where Isolde lay against her shoulder, anchoring her to the night-time world. Satiated by their love making, she didn't want to move. She'd hungered for their nights together.

"Are you tired of me yet?" Isolde slid her leg, hitching it over her wife's thigh.

Rasa chuckled, drawing the woman to her tightly, wanting a connection to as many parts of her naked body as physically possible. "There are not enough days left in our lives for me to tire of you." Her lips touched Isolde's forehead.

Pale fingertips danced across dark ribs. Isolde felt the scars pebbling her lover's skin. "We have been fighting alone for a very long time and we are not the same anymore."

Rasa stilled Isolde's hand against her abdomen. "Nothing can change what we did to survive," she whispered.

"I have done so many things." Isolde pushed up to look into Rasabel's eyes. "You wear physical scars from enemies you could see."

"Those aren't all from the last two years, my love."

Isolde ached, needing to share her darkest fears. "I could not bear it if you looked at me with shame."

Rasa reversed their positions, her biceps flexing as she hovered above her wife. "You don't know, and I don't know, what was done for survival. I ask for compassion, but not forgiveness, because I regret nothing that got us here."

Isolde grasped her lover's arms. "Nothing?"

"I am a warrior, more than I was when we first met," Rasa explained, her eyes never leaving Isolde's. "But no foe was ever like the one inside of me. The solitary days were impossible and I feared I would not survive."

"Bel." Isolde felt her lover's tears hit her face. "Did you think of leaving me?"

"Never!" Rasa's answer was absolute. "It was my worst fear that for reasons beyond my control I would not be able to stay."

"I couldn't rest without you," Isolde said. "The nights…"

Rasa's hips dipped between Isolde's parted legs. "We have been existing. That looks very different when you are only half alive."

"I don't feel quite whole," Isolde confessed.

Rasa dipped her head, peppering her wife's neck with featherlight kisses. "Oh love, I have dreamed of our bodies together like this. That somehow we would be as we were, but we are not."

Isolde felt the rise of desire as her wife's muscled body moved against hers. "You have changed."

"As have you, but even without the curse it would have happened." Rasa whispered reassurance. "We have endured. Our love has stood against the impossible and here we are."

Isolde's hand slid between their bodies, searching to fulfill the covenant of their bond. "Yes," she hissed as her fingers found their target, "here we are."

~~~~~~~~~~

"We have more than twenty coppers." Isolde hummed, the pleasure of their lovemaking seasoning her voice.

Rasa chuckled, knowing the coins were stolen and aware love accompanied their theft. "Exactly twenty-four coppers, courtesy of our little thief."

"And yet we lay on the ground of a forest wrapped in this tattered rag." Isolde chuckled, knowing her wife would take slight offense at the word.

"After all this time you are still calling it that?"

"Every night." Isolde's voice trembled, thinking about her transformations. "When I became aware, I found this"—she tugged the fabric—"folded next to Onyx's saddle."
~~~~~~~~~~

She pushed herself onto her elbow for a better view of Rasa's reaction. "You left it for me. You made little pillows and foraged for food, and every night for two years I knew that somewhere inside the wolf that showed up in my camp was the woman I needed so desperately."

"Is," Rasa rasped. "I didn't know what else to do."

"You knew exactly what to do, and you did it." Isolde smiled. "You kept us going."

"We kept our love alive," Rasa corrected. "I guarded you and you guarded me."

"Yes," Isolde agreed.

"I suppose it is good that I trained you so well," Rasa teased.

"Yes, it is very good." Isolde hummed.

They lay together, listening to the sounds of the night, Isolde coming to trust they could move on together. "What will we do now?" she asked.

"Live, my love," Rasa whispered against her hair. "Now we shall live."

The End

Publishing is not a solo journey and there are many people to thank.

To David, Victoria and David, you are everything. When I need to disappear, you are steadfast supporters of my wish for solitude. I am grateful for your voices, your kindness and always for understanding. You know what this love story means to me.

Roz and Rach, it feels impossible that we have chosen each other as family for almost half my life. I cherish your support and editing skills but most of all I cherish the people you've become. Thank you for being a part of my life journey.

Mickie, Isa, Peg and Paula, you are the best alpha team I could ask for, and your continued support keeps me going through the wild days. Thank you for every kind word, for being there and for giving me a reason to ride that train.

Jen and Donna, few people understand the grit and grime of self publishing and I don't know how I lucked out finding you. I am grateful for your honesty and even the quips. You feel like family.

Hill, thank you for always showing up.

To my mom, I hope I didn't screw up a cherished memory. I'll miss you always and I don't like my normal without you in it.

SAPPHIC BOOKS BY
SHARON K. ANGELICI

The Alice and Violet Series

Yule Be Home For Solstice
(An Alice and Violet story)

Violet and Alice's December road trip is definitely a trial by transport as they set out to deliver the perfect Yule log for the Solstice celebration. This cross-state drive commemorates twenty years of sapphic bliss and three hundred thousand miles on their Subaru Outback named Bess. What happens between home and Aunt Eunice's house is a romantic comedy of errors. Sit back and enjoy this *Planes, Trains, and Automobiles*-style adventure to deliver the perfect Yule log for Winter Solstice.

Double Dyno
Prequel to Yule Be Home For Solstice,
(An Alice and Violet story)

On a two-week hiking and climbing tour, Al Hadley guides a small team toward high adventure. With her best friends PB and Britt making up the Extreme Adventure Group, the goal is to build confidence and experience for each client. What they weren't counting on was Violet Crest and her amateur adventuring ways.

Weeks of planning and detailed maps can't tame Violet's curious nature. She's determined to make every moment count by capturing as many as possible through her camera lens, testing the boundaries and the patience of AEG's team leader, Al.

<u>Rage Room Romance Series</u>

Conned
(Book 1)

For Ella Eastman, firefighting is life. She's devoted her body to being the best, but everyone needs a break from reality once in a while. For Morgan Hail, art is life, but she has to make a living. Their lives collide when television fandoms intersect at The Blacktree Comic Palooza.

Morgan's captivating fanart leads to a heated misunderstanding, and a cosplay contest brings these two women together–though only one of them knows the truth. This unlikely pair heats up when their real-world lives collide, but what will happen to their budding romance when Ella reveals her secret identity? And can they find a way to make things work when Ella's job hits a little too close to home? Conned is a story of love, loss, new beginnings, and fandom.

DECONSTRUCTED
(Book 2:)

After eight years, Ella Eastman has a plan to create the perfect marriage proposal for her partner, Morgan. Inspired by Morgan's to-be-read pile, Ella struggles to incorporate her favorite romance tropes while asking the big question. The ideas pile up, as do the failed attempts to create their once-in-a-lifetime memory. How do you give the perfect partner the perfect memory of a perfect proposal? For Ella, it all seems to come together quite imperfectly. Revisit the Rage Room Romance's chosen family as they unite for Operation Perfect Proposal.

<u>The Maker Series</u>

MARK OF THE MAKER
(BOOK 1 OF THE MAKER SERIES)

Wildwood Blackstone believed her dream of being a country blacksmith was coming true. When the town of Bannock hires her to restore their abandoned carriage house built in the 1800s, she can't wait to begin.

But there are more than ghosts in Bannock and shortly after her arrival, she discovers this truth. When a childhood friend answers a call for help, Wildwood finds a part of her past that she longed to rediscover. Together they reveal Bannock's secret and uncover the Mark of the Maker.

THE MAGICK AND THE MAKER
(BOOK 2 OF THE MAKER SERIES)

Wildwood Blackstone longed for a life as a small-town blacksmith. She didn't imagine monsters or magick, and she never expected to fall in love with Shay.

Book two of the Maker Series finds the two women tangled together in the dark secrets buried deep in Bannock's small-town history. Is their commitment strong enough to carry them through? Who is the keeper of the Magick? When will Wildwood and Shay uncover the mystery behind the Mark of the Maker?

THE ORIGIN OF THE MAKER
(BOOK 3 OF THE MAKER SERIES)

Wildwood and her girlfriend Shay have uncovered Brigid's secret hidden deep in the earth.

Who is the stranger in the carriage house? How are they there? What do they know about the secret and the power it holds? Can Wildwood and Shay find the answers and keep fighting the monsters hunting them night and day?

THE LEGACY OF THE MAKER
(BOOK 4 OF THE MAKER SERIES)

In a secret world filled with magick, Wildwood Blackstone has encountered unbelievable mysteries. As the blacksmith in her new hometown, she's survived and endured the call to wield the hammer of the goddess Brigid, but to what end?

Celebrating a year with her girlfriend, Shay, the two continue their search for answers. What lived inside Andrea Peters? How did the entity survive for hundreds of years? Who controlled her all this time?

Their call to be The Magick and The Maker of Bannock comes with more questions than ever, but it might also come with answers to their past. Wildwood and Shay are drawn into endless realms, all of which lead to the Legacy of the Maker.

MORE BOOKS BY
SHARON K. ANGELICI

DEAR KANE; WHAT I WISH WE WOULD HAVE SAID

Do the words that we say in front of our children build them up or tear them down? This short story explores the consequences of hatred and bigotry when it applies, unknowingly, to someone that you love. There's a time in every relationship when a parent must let go of the dreams they have for their child, so the child can chase what they dream to become.

IMMORTAL HUMAN TRUTH

Immortal Human Truth is a collection of poetry written by the author as she traveled to promote her first book *Dear Kane; What I wish we would have said*. Each section explores experiences with love, injustice, loss, and triumph of the spirit.

SHE BELIEVED SHE COULD

What can you do in a single day? Why haven't you done it yet? Jump out of your comfort zone and dive into life as you follow the author on her journey to achieve 365 new experiences in 365 days.

ABOUT THE AUTHOR

Sharon K. Angelici, she/her, was born in the American Midwest, but her heart and soul belong to the mountains of Colorado.

She began writing as a child, using words to recover from trauma-induced depression. As a member of the LGBTQ+ community, she's an advocate for depression awareness and suicide prevention. In 2016 she published her first book dealing with both subjects, *Dear Kane; what I wish we would have said.*

Sharon is a full-time lover of life and all things Pagan and Magick. She's an artist and blacksmith, which inspired her to create her Maker series.